# SECTS AND THE CITY

## STEFON MEARS

Thousand
Faces
Publishing

# Also by Stefon Mears

*Cavan Oltblood Series*
*Half a Wizard*
*The Ice Dagger*
*Spells of Undeath*

**Spells for Hire**
*Devil's Shoestring*
*Zombie Powder*
*Spirit Trap*
*Dragon's Blood*

**The Rise of Magic**
*Magician's Choice*
*Sleight of Mind*
*Lunar Alchemy*
*Three Fae Monte*
*The Sphinx Principle*
*Double Backed Magic*

**The Telepath Trilogy**
*Surviving Telepathy*
*Immoral Telepathy*
*Targeting Telepathy*

**Edge of Humanity**
*Caught Between Monsters*
*Hunting Monsters*

**Power City Tales**
*Not Quite Bulletproof*
*No Money in Heroism*

*Sects and the City*
*Prince of a Thousand Worlds (coming soon)*
*Longhairs and Short Tales: A Collection of Cat Stories*
*Devil's Night*
*Portal-Land, Oregon*
*Stealing from Pirates*
*Fade to Gold*
*With a Broken Sword*
*Twice Against the Dragon*
*The House on Cedar Street*
*Sudden Death*
*On the Edge of Faerie*
*Confronting Legends (Spells & Swords Vol. 1)*
*Uncle Stone Teeth and Other Macabre Poems*
*The Patreon Collection, Vol. 1-5 (Vol. 6, coming soon)*

Published by Thousand Faces Publishing, Portland, Oregon

http://1kfaces.com



ISBN: 978-1-948490-21-4

# Sects and the City

1

---

# CLARK

Well, the world didn't end, so I had to open the bar.

Didn't really expect the world to end, you understand. I mean, that sort of thing doesn't usually happen on a Tuesday night, when the moon is nothing special, and there aren't even any shooting stars, much less a comet of ill omen.

Here's the thing, though. The way the gruesome foursome had been talking lately, I thought it might really happen this time.

Most of the people who come into my bar, Zoth, are the kind who treat occultism as a game. Play stuff, like horror movies and the stories Lovecraft published.

Heck, there are even two live-action roleplaying game crews who run their campaigns here on Thursdays and Saturdays.

My little east side bar is the toast of Portland's weirdos.

And I mean that affectionately. After all, I'm one of the weirdos, and they're the clientele I was aiming for when I opened Zoth two years ago.

Even decorated with them in mind. Matte black for the walls, floor and ceiling, but with symbols from the Simon *Necronomicon* books done in dayglow colors here and there, and lit up with black lights for extra funk.

Posters on the walls from horror movies with a heavy emphasis on Lovecraft adaptations like *Re-Animator*, *Dagon*, and *The Resurrected*. Even have an original poster from *The Haunted Place* behind the bar next to the crowning jewel of my décor.

A shoggoth in a jar.

All right, it's just a gelatin mixture made with a blend of oils and glycerin in a suspension that's mostly water. But with its stand rotating under its own black light, it looks like a shifting mass of something you can't quite see.

Great conversation piece, for the right kind of people.

I've got two big rooms done this way, connected by wide hallways that feel like continuations of the rooms. Wraparound bar in the middle, with a small kitchen, so I can serve my patrons anywhere they hang out. Tables in the back, dancing in the front.

For the music, I play a lot of old goth stuff mostly. Bauhaus. Siouxsie and the Banshees. Sisters of Mercy. Dead Can Dance. But I mix in some Darkest of the Hillside Thickets, to go with the general theme.

I don't play the music too loud, either. People actually like to talk in my bar.

Which brings me back to the gruesome foursome.

First of all, I never call them that aloud. Last thing I want to do is offend one of those guys.

See, those four, they take their occultism very seriously, with a heavy emphasis on the *cult*. Guys like these are the *basis* for horror films. And the stories Lovecraft *didn't* publish.

They started coming in about six months ago. Every Wednesday, like clockwork. They creep me the fuck out, but they tip well.

Plus, on Wednesdays, they were my whole lunch rush. Which I had to hope was coincidence.

I was thinking about them as I opened up that day. Wondering if they'd be in. If they'd be pissed that the world hadn't ended. Or ... rather, if *one* of them would be pissed. The one whose crew was supposed to end it.

See, far as I can tell, they're all cultists, but they're part of different cults.

Which one was talking about the world ending last night?

Couldn't remember. I'd been too busy doing inventory when I'd heard that key phrase: "and the world shall end at last."

They didn't come back to it, unfortunately. And it didn't feel like the kind of thing I could come up and ask about.

So I let Frank close up for me last night, and spent the night with Cindy, my sometimes girlfriend. Just in case.

I unlocked the back door at the crack of noon that day. Flipped on the saddest thing ever.

The regular lights of a bar.

A bar under regular lights just looks sad. Or at least mine did. Like seeing a clown without makeup, or that one lonely guy at the end of the bar, casting about desperately for someone to go home with when he hears those fatal words, "last call."

The night cleaning crew did a good job though. Floors, tables, bar, bathrooms. I could even smell the lemon of their cleaner, rather than spilled beer, or something worse.

Hey. Even weirdos sometimes throw up in bar bathrooms.

But the night cleaning crew did good. This made three days in a row I didn't have to tear their shift lead a new one. If they went a whole week, well, getting them a cake could be interpreted as sarcasm. But I'd come up with something.

I threw together a grilled cheddar on sourdough from the block of Tillamook I kept for myself in the fridge, and washed it down with water while I double-checked the beer taps.

One of them was clogged. No cake for the night cleaning crew then. It was the Guinness tap, too, which sucked, because one of the gruesome foursome liked his beers thick and dark. Like his life.

Otherwise, the flow lines were good, and everything was together behind the bar. I still had about a dozen things to do — not the least of which was double-checking the night's receipts — but I needed to open up if I wanted to make any money that day.

And my bills didn't pay themselves.

I shut down the sad lights and turned on the regular bar lights — dim in most places, but black lights where they counted.

I thought about putting on some music, but didn't. I'd put some on if I got enough customers, but if it was the just the gruesome foursome again, well, I wanted to eavesdrop.

I unlocked and threw open the front door, hissed against the spring air and sunlight — purely for effect, you understand — and let it close again.

I flipped on the neon "open" sign.

Didn't even reach the bar before the first member of the gruesome foursome came in.

<hr>

I was about halfway across the dance floor, on my way back to my station behind the bar, when the door opened and my first customer came in.

Eamon, in his usual uniform — black long-sleeved shirt, buttoned up all the way (much like his personality), black jeans, black belt, black loafers. He kept his hair black, and cut short enough to show off his widow's peak.

For the first month that Eamon came in, I thought he was one of the vampire wannabes. He had the pale and skinny look down pat, like he was three years out of undergrad and still sleeping in a coffin in his mother's basement. Even wore the kind of cologne I associated with the vamp wannabes — subtle and exotic.

But that silver chain around his neck didn't hold an ankh. It held a goat's head inside an inverted pentacle. And the only times he talked about blood, he was either talking about magic or sacrifices.

Not to say he never drank any. Don't really know.

I *was* pretty sure by now that Eamon was a Satanist. Well, maybe not a *Satan* Satanist, but something along those lines.

"Salutations, Clark," he said. "A bottle of Teufelsbrau red and one of your fine cheeseburgers, extra rare."

Didn't need to ask what kind of cheese. He always wanted swiss. But one thing he did vary.

"Sure thing, Eamon. Fries today?"

"No. Onion rings."

He proceeded straight to their regular table at the back of the back.

I'd just gotten his food going when I heard someone else come in. I poked my head out of the kitchen to see the next member of the gruesome foursome arrive.

Harley.

He *looked* like any of the guys you might see on their way to a Timbers game. Plaid flannel shirt — blue today — over blue jeans. Shaggy brown hair and even shaggier brown beard. Big guy, too. Like he should've been riding his namesake.

Real backwoods vibe. Even carried a strong scent of outdoors with him. But there was always something else underneath that smell of trees and dirt. Something alkali, and slightly unwholesome. Off-putting.

From little things I'd heard him say, Harley was part of a sect that worshiped the *actual* Cthulhu.

Yeah. I used to think those stories were all fiction too. I sometimes long for those blissfully ignorant days...

Harley was grumbling when he looked up at me, and I thought his dark eyes looked angry. Might've been his folks failing their Armageddon test last night.

"Fried tentacles," he said by way of a greeting, "and sour mash whiskey. Lots of it."

No Guinness for him today? Must've been my lucky day. I mean, even apart from the world not ending.

I threw some calamari in the fryer for him — "fried tentacles" was my menu listing for calamari — and poured him a double. I slid it along the bar to him as he reached the back room. He caught the drink, tossed it back, and zinged the glass back to me.

I poured him another double, and this one he carried to the table where Eamon was already waiting.

Zed was the next one in.

They say that serial killers look just like everyone else. If so, Zed might've been one. Seen the guy every Wednesday for six months and I still might not've been able to pick him out of a lineup.

Zed was short and slight. Not too pale. Hair such a nondescript brown that I didn't even remember what color his hair was, the first month he came in.

Hell, I introduced myself to Zed three times. Three. And part of the reason my regulars are regulars is that I never forget a name or a face.

Maybe I just wish I could forget Zed. Far as I was concerned, he was the creepiest of the lot.

Part of that, I think, was that he didn't seem to have any smell at all. I mean not even a cheap deodorant or anything.

But even beyond his lack of odor, there was just something off about him. Something *wrong*. Like the air itself didn't want to touch him.

It was springtime, and the Blazers were in the playoffs. So Zed's human camouflage had him wearing a Damian Lillard tee shirt and cargo shorts, along with simple leather sandals.

I had no idea what the hell Zed worshiped, and I kind of hoped I never found out. I only knew he was part of something because I occasionally heard his quiet voice say something along the lines of "the others say" or "we have something planned for tonight."

"Clark Phillips."

Even hearing Zed say my name gave me a chill. Like he was reminding me he knew my name, where I lived, and probably where my parents lived. Just in case he ever needed the information.

I had to clear my throat to speak to Zed. Always had to.

"How you doing, Zed?"

No answer to the question, of course. Just the most nondescript order he could place.

"Burger with fries. Pabst Blue Ribbon."

He continued on to his table.

All three of their meals were ready by the time Sebastian came rolling in.

I smiled despite myself when Sebastian entered the bar. He just had that kind of effect on people. He was tall, blonde, gently muscled and movie-star handsome, with a perpetual smile on his lips and in his blue, blue eyes.

Tell you something. I've always thought of myself as straight. But if Sebastian hit on me, I don't know if I could say no. I don't know if anyone could. He just had this aura of vibrant sexuality to him.

Anyway, he was dressed for the heat. Soft brown Utilikilt over well-broken-in leather sandals. He wore a blue tee shirt that matched his eyes. Its material was too shiny to be cotton, but I didn't think it was silk.

Like with Zed, I had no idea what Sebastian worshiped. Unlike with Zed, Sebastian's cult might tempt me.

"Pleasure to see you, Clark," he said in a rich baritone, "as always."

He stopped just across the bar from me, close enough that I could detect his insinuation of a cologne. Masculine, subtle and enticing.

"What'll you have, Sebastian?"

His eyes flicked over me for a moment in a way that made me feel as though I was on the menu and under consideration.

Mind you, Sebastian was only twenty-two — which made him a decade younger than me. Plus, you know, he was a *guy*. A member of the sex that had never been my personal brand of whisky.

But damn if my heart didn't beat a little faster as he made and held eye contact while ordering.

"Chili burger with extra cheddar," he said, as though sharing a dirty, intimate secret. "A side of chili cheese fries. And to drink ... a chocolate daiquiri. Extra whipped cream."

Where the hell he put it all I had no idea.

I hustled to get his order together, and not just because it was for Sebastian.

I had the distinct feeling they were going to talk about something important today. And I needed to hear what.

———

THE GRUESOME FOURSOME WERE QUIET AS I BROUGHT SEBASTIAN HIS indulgent lunch.

"Sure you don't want some water with that?"

Sebastian just smiled and shook his head while picking up a french fry dripping with chili and cheese. I averted my eyes before the fry made it to his lips.

"Anyone ready for refills?"

Eamon and Harley were ready for more Teufelsbrau red and sour mash whiskey, respectively, but Zed had barely touched his PBR.

They didn't start the serious conversation until I'd returned with their refills. And when they started in, I started working on the spigot for the Guinness tap. Mostly for the excuse to be in listening range.

"I take it," Sebastian asked Harley in a lazy voice, "all did not go as planned last night?"

"A bunch of fucking Carters busted in, right as we were getting to the good part."

"Carter" was a term I'd heard them use a few times over the prior six months. At first, I'd thought it was a pejorative of some sort. Over time, through context, I decided that it had to refer to some kind of counter-cult.

Though whether "Carter" was a title, or just the surname common to a family that seemed to oppose all of the gruesome four-some's cult activities, I couldn't be sure.

If it was one family, though, they kept pretty busy.

"No sacrifice then?" Sebastian asked, and I thought maybe he was teasing.

"I don't even want to talk about it. Not yet." Harley downed his whole glass of sour mash and slammed the empty down on the table. "Another!"

"Maybe you should switch to beer," Eamon said. "You would not wish to be inebriated if the call comes."

Harley glared at Eamon until Eamon's ears pinked.

"Excuse me," Eamon said. "Unfortunate choice of words. But the intended sentiment remains valid. If your high priest—"

"High priest*ess*," Sebastian corrected, toying with his glass. "And a delectable thing she is, too."

"She'd kill you," Harley growled.

"Might not be a bad way to go," Sebastian mused.

"Eamon's point remains," Zed said, softly. "If you will consume at this rate, you should consider a beverage lighter in alcohol."

"Unless you want to switch teams," Sebastian said with an inviting smile.

"Ah ah," Eamon said, admonishing Sebastian with a waggling finger. "What's the core agreement of these meetings?"

"No proselytizing," they all said together.

"Fine," Harley said with a sigh. Then, louder, continued, "Clark, a Guinness instead of the whiskey."

"Tap's clogged," I said with a grimace. "I can get you a bottle."

Sebastian whistled long and loud like he was calling a dog from far afield. Zed turned a sharp glare on him.

"Try it now," Sebastian said.

I won't deny my expression was suspicious as I picked up a glass and tested the tap. The tap that had been clogged shut when I came in. A clog I'd barely gotten started on.

Tap poured just as smooth as it was supposed to on its best day.

All three of the others were glaring at Sebastian when I brought Harley his Guinness. As I walked back to the bar, I heard him say, "Hey. You guys wanted to meet in a *bar*. Sometimes that means I have duties I can't ignore."

It was the most serious thing Sebastian had ever said, and it gave me the shivers. And not for any sexual reason.

The others seemed to grudgingly accept his statement, and settled back to their food and drinks.

"For what it's worth," Sebastian said, "I've had a bad week as well."

"Me too," Eamon said, frowning. "And yet, I'd read nothing in the conjunctions that spoke of forces moving against any of us, much less against each of us. Am I alone in this?"

"All had appeared clear," Zed said, while the others echoed the sentiment. "And yet, we ... had our difficulties as well."

All four pondered that over their drinks.

"Perhaps, if we each discussed our ... difficulties," Eamon said, "we could find common inhibitors, and work together to clear them."

"I'd welcome some help dealing with the Carters," Harley said, then drank down half his beer in one pull.

"Your suggestion," Sebastian said, somehow understandable despite his mouth full of chili cheeseburger.

"Very well," Eamon said. "I shall begin."

2
———

# EAMON

I FIND THAT THE PROPERLY ORGANIZED MIND DOES NOT MAKE EXCESSIVE use of patterns. To become too predictable is to fall in line with the desires and goals of the Great Oppressor, who would keep us all as little more than blind sheep, following his designated shepherds to our inevitable doom.

Freedom, of course, is the path of He Whom We Follow. And that freedom, as well, suggests avoiding an overreliance on conditioned habituation.

*"You risk edging toward proselytization," Zed said.*

I am aware of our rules, and I shall not tread upon them. But in explaining the events of Friday, I must begin with their under-pinnings.

What I have to tell you will mean nothing, unless you first understand that I eschew excessive repetitions of behavior as crutches of the disorganized mind.

There are exceptions, of course, or the mere avoidance of patterns becomes a pattern unto itself, and thus, a weakness.

My meetings with you three are one such exception, and my daily awakening is another.

The majority of my brethren and sistren sleep the day away and do their work at night, when the power of He Whom We Follow is at its zenith.

I choose to rise each day with the sun and do my work while His power is at its nadir. This might make my tasks more difficult, but when I succeed I find it ever so much more rewarding.

And it was this very habit — if I might be allowed so droll a colloquialism — that afforded me a rare opportunity this past Friday.

I arose at six-twenty in the morning, precisely with the dawn. I will spare you the details of my ablutions, but I took my morning run before breaking my fast.

I costume myself as one of the sheep when I go running. I wear red athletic shorts and a gray tee shirt, white socks and running shoes. I don no jewelry.

Where I live, out where the fertile hunting grounds that border Portland's suburbia encroach on the farmlands of old, the grounds are flat enough that I may run freely on the streets without drawing unwanted attention.

The streets are wide, and often without sidewalks. The firs compete for nutrients with oaks and Japanese maples, magnolia trees and blossoming cherries.

The houses crouch, as though watching the battle of the trees, and placing their bets on who shall emerge victorious.

The green of their overwatered lawns provides a delightful mockery of a battlefield. Cars move along the streets infrequently at that hour, as though running bets to the bookmaker.

Moving among those trees and issuing their cries of territorial challenge fly the other combatants of our neighborhood. The crows and the western meadowlarks.

They rarely do direct battle, those birds. However, their chattering about their dominance is louder through the streets of my neighborhood than the distant traffic at that hour.

By the time I would truly head home, more people will be on their way to work, and the unhappy growling of their vehicles shall outstrip the morning birds.

But as I started out that morning, the birds had a solid auditory lead.

The morning air carried a challenging chill that Friday, as though daring me to wait for the sun to rise higher and heat my body for me.

I contemplated that air as I began my run, to the north, and wove among the blocks, turning whenever inspiration struck me.

I had fallen into a meditative reverie on the contrast between cold morning air and the warmth inside my nostrils, when I realized I smelled something abnormal.

The typical smells of my morning runs — when I take them — include grass and trees, rain, when appropriate, and gasoline when cars are thick on the ground or when the lawnmowers run rampant. And, of course, my own sweat after the first several minutes.

But that morning, as I turned up an unfamiliar block, I smelled something unusual. Something along the lines of ammonia, or perhaps cat urine. The odor was not strong. Had I not been focused in the manner that I was, I might have passed it by, unknowing.

Nevertheless. I have met many cats in my day. And none have ever expressed urine so powerful that I could detect it from the street, while running.

I was smelling a methamphetamine lab. I was certain of it.

I pondered that as I covered the next two blocks, with the odor fading quickly behind me. The more I considered the question, the more certain I became that I had happened upon a methamphetamine lab in the wild.

I turned then, and made my way back toward that block, as though merely returning on my run. I did not anticipate any unwelcome observation, but in this day and age, one cannot be too careful.

On this pass, I paid more attention to my surroundings.

The houses on that block had the look and feel of newer construction. They pushed closer to the street and their neighbors, with their walls, their siding all looked to have been painted within the past year or so, and none of their roofs showed any significant signs of wear. Even their doors and windowsills seemed fresh and new.

What was more, several of the houses stood two stories tall, which the older houses of the neighborhood did not.

I could practically feel jealousy seething from the houses. This was a block where recent owners competed with one another, and the older owners could only huddle and cope.

My object of my search, however, was none of those.

Near the corner on the west side, where the smell was most notable to one who paid strict attention to his olfactory input, languished an incomplete shell of a house.

Its three-story skeleton had been framed out, but no trucks full of workers parked in front, nor filled its scant, gravel driveway.

What was more, the skeleton had been exposed to the elements for too long. I could see signs of wear along the support beams.

It had the feel of a puppy cast out into the streets by a family who could no longer afford to feed it.

I was looking at someone's overambitious project. A dream they had hoped to fulfill, but a dream squashed by the inequities of waking life.

Perhaps a lost job. A family illness. An unfortunate addiction. Whatever the reason, the owner ran out of money before the house was even half-finished.

*"Did that please you?" Sebastian dared to ask. "That failure?"*

Of course not. That house, if finished, would have lorded its presence over its neighbors. A shrine to the ego of its owner. Perhaps even a personal tower of Babel.

A tragic waste, if not finished soon. By summer what remained of it would be no more enduring than Shelly's statue of Ozymandias.

But under the ambitiously lain floorboards, I knew, had to lay a methamphetamine lab. Perhaps the owner's desperate attempt to raise funds to complete the house, making it all the finer in my mind.

I had to know more.

---

THE HOUSES AROUND THE SUSPECTED METHAMPHETAMINE LAB ONLY HAD proper fences when they also had proper dogs. And I do confess. Had this shell of a house shown me a proper fence, I would have assumed the chemists downstairs were protecting their lab of ill repute with the sort of canine guardian who would be only too happy to take his afternoon meal from my flesh.

Not to say that I would have ignored said house for long, even if the site was guarded by a rottweiler or an ill-treated pit bull. However, I would have come back with ... proper measures in place to ensure my own safety during the venture.

I noted quickly enough, however, that the closest thing this house had to a fence was a line of arbor vitae. They looked several years old, and my suspicious eyes saw no sign of, to name only one possible example, a chain-linked cyclone fence hidden within their branches.

I learned the hard way once that some dog owners employ such measures. And I bear the scar on my hindquarters to prove it.

*"Truly?" Sebastian asked in that teasing tone of his. "Could I see this scar?"*

You may not. And I shall ask you to cease your interruptions, lest I subject you to similar treatment when your own turn to talk should come.

Now. Having determined that I could approach without the risk of physical fangs, I next turned my attention to possible security measures beyond the realm of the mundane.

I detected neither wards, nor guardian spirits, nor even defensive servitors. The household ahead of me appeared to be completely mundane.

And, I do confess, I allowed this fact to inspire within me a sense of security exceeding that to which I was entitled.

I double-checked my surroundings, but the nearest person visible to me was behind the wheel of a Toyota Celica two blocks down and moving away.

The crows held sway over the meadowlarks on this block. A murder of more than a dozen roosted on a nearby magnolia tree, watching me as though they expected to see something interesting.

I moved quickly across the scrubby, abused lawn to the side of the house, where the fit and firm arbor vitae would shelter me from the potential prying eyes of neighbors.

Three of the crows followed, alighting the beams of what might have become an attic, and calling out to their companions.

I ignored their cries, though, and listened hard. Hard enough that I could hear the breeze gently rustling the arbor vitae. But I heard no telltale sounds of activity from my suspected methamphetamine lab.

I frowned at the floorboards lain in support of the skeleton's "ground" floor. I'd expected them to cover only the first half of the house, but they covered all the way to the back. And I had not so much as a smartphone on my person, to provide light if needed.

I can *feel* the question that none of you are voicing, and yes, I could produce a light should I need one. But I've always considered that a vulgar display of power, and one that can be most difficult to explain, should an observer happen along at the wrong moment.

I did not expect such measures would be necessary. While cooking up methamphetamine was not the most complicated chemical procedure I could name, I did not suspect that any were so good at it that they would needlessly exercise their skill in darkness.

The grass along the side of the house was in even worse shape than it had been out front. Here it was all crabgrass and weeds. Hardly attractive, but sufficient to aid in silencing the sound of my running shoes as I picked my slow path to the back of the house.

Somewhere back there had to be a...

Ah. I spotted the stairwell at the back of the house.

Clearly the owner's finances had extended to at least digging and laying a proper foundation before construction began. I could see hard, but dirty concrete steps coming down from the edge of what — if I read the rough sketches on the floorboards correctly — might someday become the kitchen.

The backyard was all dirt. Not rich, properly poured soil, waiting for grass or Oregon native plants, either. No, it was pale dirt, with more than its share of rocks and rough clay.

I paused at the back corner of the house, where the support

beams were wide enough to do a decent job of concealing my presence.

From there, I glanced upward, to see which of the nearby houses might observe my activities, now that the crows up around the eaves had been joined by more of their compatriots. All of them chattering about something.

Two houses were close enough and tall enough that they might present a risk of exposure.

And not just for me. A woman with long, honey blonde hair wore only a very revealing nightgown as she rose and crossed her bedroom. She took no interest in the cawing of crows, nor indeed anything beyond the walls of her own house.

In neither case did either house demonstrate a threat.

I continued on. Slower now. More cautiously. At any moment someone might come up those stairs, and if so I wanted to see before I was seen.

As I reached the top of the stairs, I finally heard noise from down below. First, I heard a soft, constant, sucking sound. After a moment's consideration, I decided that was likely a propane tank providing fuel for a flame. After all, this "house" was nowhere near ready to connect to the local power grid.

Once I thought of that, I decided I could smell propane in use, underneath the stronger ammonia odor.

Beyond that, I thought I also heard movements. Perhaps shoes scraping on concrete. Soft voices too quiet for comprehension.

I crouched, to see what I might see beyond the limits of the early morning sunlight. I thought I could detect a whitish glow. Fluorescence seemed unlikely to me, but if they were using propane for their cooking, they might also use it to light their lamps.

Seemed excessively risky to me, given the potential volatility of their end product. But it spoke well, potentially, of their confidence and their skills.

If so, there might be a way we could help one another.

I drew a breath to remind my accelerating heart that I was the master of every situation, and that it should slow to its more normal pace.

With that, I mustered my forces, and made my way down the concrete stairs.

---

I CREPT SLOWLY DOWN THE STAIRS. NOT CROUCHED AND POISED FOR trouble, but upright. As though I were merely a passerby who had become curious about the fate of this structure, and whether or not anything of interest might lie underneath it.

Still, I shifted my weight on the soles of my running shoes to minimize the sounds I might make, as well as to control my descent.

The stairs were solid concrete, if dirty, but they lacked a rail. Once my head came below the line of the main floor's floorboards, I would have nothing to grab onto, should one of the stairs prove less solid than it appeared.

I reached the bottom safely.

Down here the ammonia smell was so strong as to be overpowering, and the propane odor not far behind it.

Standing down here, now, amid such stench, I wondered that none of the neighbors had complained. Which should've been my second warning.

*"At the risk of incurring your ire," Sebastian said with more sarcasm than I cared for, "Second?"*

I shall come to it. Now. Down here was not the wide open concrete basement that I expected. Rather instead, someone had used floorboards to form crude walls that hung like curtains, nailed haphazardly to the support beams of the main floor above.

The walls formed a hallway that continued to the back of the basement, where they stopped short, forming something of a tee intersection.

I could see light coming through the cracks between the hanging walls, as well as underneath them, and more light and shadows down at the intersection.

The light was pale, and I felt more certain than ever that propane provided it. I could hear the suction of propane to either side of my little corridor, as well as muffled voices coming from the left-hand side.

I mouthed the word "hello" without giving any voice to it. That would serve to give the ring of truth to my words when I asked if anyone heard when I called out a greeting upon reaching the basement.

I proceeded down the corridor in silence. Listening, but as yet unable to comprehend the conversation of those people beyond my left-hand wall. I felt confident that I was hearing English, but the suction of the propane tanks roared like jet engines, by way of comparison. Whoever they were, they must've been accustomed to speaking *sotto voce*, to avoid drawing attention from the world above.

I could pick out three distinct voices, all of which sounded more likely male than female. Or at least somewhere the male side of neutral, when considering the entire spectrum of potential genders.

*"Thank you for that,"* Sebastian said.

You are welcome. Now, then.

Although certain I heard propane on the right-hand side as well — though the tight echoes of the basement made this questionable — I was equally certain that I heard no voices on that side. I speculated that the area to my right was used for sleeping quarters, or at least as an employee lounge, while business was conducted on the left-hand side.

A notion of which, I must say, I approved.

I did not approve of all that ammonia in the air, though. I had not yet broken my fast for the day, and the ammonia was leaving a poor taste in my mouth. As well as a discomforting feeling in my eyes and nostrils, just short of burning.

I finally reached the intersection at the end of the makeshift corridor, and did the most natural thing in the world, for an adherent to the example of He Whom We Follow.

I took the left-hand path.

This side of the basement was hemmed in by concrete, and little more than thrice the width of the makeshift corridor.

Closest to me I saw a cheap card table, with equally cheap chairs. Both table and chairs currently empty. Along the walls, I saw the methamphetamine laboratory itself, arrayed among two much sturdier, collapsible tables made from heavy, durable plastic.

The cooking was indeed done by propane, fed from a big Blue Hippo-brand tank. A second such tank fed the propane camp lantern, which supplied the light.

Cardboard banker boxes lay in stacks against the crude, hanging wall. I could only assume they contained either supplies or product. Perhaps both.

I wasn't concerned enough about the boxes to check them. I was far more concerned about the fact that I seemed to be alone on this side of the basement, despite my plainly having heard voices coming from over here.

The warning came at last. A ruffling at the back of my neck, and a twitching in my solar plexus. Both strong indications of imminent danger.

I turned to make good my escape, but before I could take even a single step back into the makeshift corridor, properly inverted pentacles flared to bright green life in five, surrounding places on the concrete of the implied room.

Too late.

The trap had been sprung. And I was inside it.

## 3

# CLARK

The gruesome foursome lapsed into tense silence as I brought a round of refills. Another Teufelsbrau red for Eamon, a Guinness for Harley, and another chocolate daiquiri with extra cream for Sebastian.

Zed was still working on his first Pabst Blue Ribbon, which the others seemed to notice as I set down their drinks. They glared at him. He made a show of taking a long pull from his beer.

Sebastian, who had been entertaining himself by doodling on the table in spilled salt, opened his mouth to say something.

Harley spoke first, pointing at Zed.

"He'll have another beer."

Sweat beaded on my forehead. Maybe I needed to get the air conditioning going early today. Unusual for spring.

No, I realized as I made eye contact with the depth of darkness that was Zed. It's just them. Maybe they radiated heat. Or maybe they just made me nervous.

I had to clear my throat to say something, even though I'd gone through two glasses of water while eavesdropping on Eamon's story.

"Bar policy," I said apologetically and shrugged for emphasis. "I need you to confirm you want another round."

"Yes," Zed said in a flat tone as he set down his can. "I would like a second Pabst Blue Ribbon."

I wedged a smile onto my face, and tried to pretend it looked like something other than a rictus grin.

"Can I bring you boys anything else?"

"More fried tentacles," Harley said.

"Some jalapeño poppers for the table," Eamon said.

"I would like..." Sebastian rolled his lips around as he thought, holding eye contact with me the whole time. With one hand he brushed away his doodles.

Definitely. I definitely needed to get the AC going.

"Yes," Sebastian finally said. "I would like a slice of your thickest, richest chocolate cake, with a scoop of vanilla ice cream. Drizzle the whole thing with hot chocolate, if you would."

"We don't have cake," I said, irritated that disappointing Sebastian made me feel bad. "We do have some pretty good brownies. And we have the ice cream and chocolate sauce. I could heat the brownie and the sauce, if you like."

"Make it two brownies, then," Sebastian said with a languorous smile. "With one large scoop of vanilla, and lots and lots of chocolate sauce. Heated, if you'd be so kind."

"You got it," I said, hating myself for the wide smile that lit my face. "I don't have regular cherries, but I can put a maraschino cherry on it, if you like."

"Never in my life have I refused a cherry," he said with a smile full of insinuation.

I quickly turned to Zed. "Anything more for you?"

"Just the Pabst Blue Ribbon."

I nodded and made my escape to get their food ready.

I was nearly back behind the bar when I heard them start talking again.

"So," Harley said. "Before you get back into it, my question's the same as pleasure boy's. You said the strong odor in the basement was the second warning sign. What was the first?"

"I would prefer to explain that in retrospect," Eamon said, "rather than interrupt the flow of my narrative for purposes of enlightenment."

"I should like to hear the answer too," Zed said. "I suspect it'll give us a better perspective on your experience as it unfolds."

"Oh, very well."

I stopped behind the bar, leaned down, and fiddled with ... nothing important. Just for an excuse to avoid going into kitchen now and missing the answer.

Basically I rearranged a few glasses, hoping it sounded like sorting through beer bottles.

"The crows were the first warning sign."

"Crows are everywhere in the greater Portland area," Zed said, while the other two murmured agreement.

"Yes," Eamon agreed. "And I do not refer to the crows I passed on my run, nor those who hung about on the street."

"The crows that joined you at the house," Harley said.

"Those very same," Eamon said. "They alighted the skeleton of the house as though it were commonplace for them. And yet, the floorboards below them — floorboards that had been exposed to ample opportunity for some time — remained steadfastly bare of bird excrement."

"So they weren't in the *habit* of hanging out on the house structure," Sebastian said.

"Not in the least. Nor were any of their brethren, nor, indeed, any birds at all."

Eamon paused for a sip of beer while his compatriots absorbed that.

"Yes," he said. "It should have been obvious that they followed me to the house to cry a warning to those who worked below."

Now, I hadn't heard any of them ask a question. But for all I knew he was answering a question one of them had asked telepathically. I wasn't discounting anything at this point. Not after the crack about him being able to produce visible light by what could only be magic.

Real. Magic.

Not story stuff. The real thing. Which meant that *he* was the real thing. Which meant that *all four of them* were the real thing.

Yeah, I'd suspected for a while now that those three had something real going. Just little hints, like the fact that no one else ever came into my bar when they were here. Not even to use the facilities.

And the timing of my Guinness tap just unclogging itself was pretty darned convenient, if I say so myself.

But that light thing. He wasn't talking about some LED flashlight on his key chain. And the flaring pentacles Eamon described, those could only mean he'd been trapped by magic.

He was throwing all this out there so casually he might've been talking about traffic throwing off the schedule of the MAX light rail train.

And the others just ... nodded along. Like nothing he was saying surprised or shocked any of them.

Like maybe they could produce light from nothing too. And maybe they could all lay magical booby traps. And maybe do who else knew what.

All of which meant that just maybe the world really did almost end last night.

My stomach felt like it wanted to run out the back door, turn south, and keep running until it hit the end of Argentina. I shivered like I was freezing, but I felt sweaty all over.

My hands shook, as I hurried into the kitchen to prep their food.

These were not people to keep waiting.

Plus, terrified as I was right then, I knew I had to hear more.

4

# EAMON

Hubris has brought down greater men than I, of which there have never been many.

My hubris that day lay in ignoring the warning signs, true, but only tertiarily.

My secondary act of hubris had preceded even those warning signs that day.

When I had paused to examine the property that concealed the methamphetamine laboratory, I looked for wards, as I should have. I also cast about, in case there were guardian spirits of any sort. Demons or elementals, perhaps, or even specially constructed servitor spirits.

I felt certain that anyplace that could possibly pose a threat to my person must, logically, have such defenses of its own in place. Elsewise they would risk a potential enemy sending in a scout, or even devastating them with an attack, without the least fear of failure or retribution.

I should have looked to see if there were any spells at all lain about the place. Even potential spells, those that lay not active, but waiting to be triggered.

*"Are you good at spotting those?" Harley asked, with sufficient respect in his voice that I considered responding with only a smile.*

Good enough. Though I admit it would have taken even me more time to determine, with certainty, what lay waiting below. Sufficient time that I would have risked being spotted by a curious neighbor.

Which, of course, might have led to questions, and clean up, and significantly more effort than I had intended to expend that morning.

The reason it would have taken so much time, you see, was that they whose spells lay in that basement had expended effort to conceal what they had prepared. Sufficient effort to preclude the casual detection of even those who have trained to the extent that we have.

That fact was what I should have recognized when the crows came a-cawing. And when the odors of ammonia and propane become so much more pronounced once I reached the basement floor.

Had I recognized those things, I would have evaded the issue entirely. I would have assigned the site its proper level of threat, and taken a far more cautious, time-intensive approach. Likely beginning with online research about the property while issuing an investigatory servitor to inspect the location in my place.

Although it must be admitted that with less risk, comes less reward...

Now, before we were interrupted by our bartender, I had been saying that the pentacles flared bright green.

*"You haven't told us your primary hubris yet," Sebastian said.*

No. I have not. I shall come to that at the appropriate time, if necessary, though I suspect it shall become most obvious well before I finish.

Now. If I may.

I had come down the stairs into the concrete basement of that skeleton of a house. Clad in nothing more than my running gear, including appropriate footwear. I wore no jewelry. I carried no special charms. I had about my person, only such defenses as I keep up at all times. Those which are necessary to live our lives as we four do.

In short, I was as close to unarmed and defenseless as I am ever likely to get.

I had passed between those rough walls of a makeshift corridor, and turned left at the end, following what I believed to have been a conversation of three men, speaking in low voices.

Around that turn I had found the source of those noisome ammonia and propane stenches: the methamphetamine laboratory.

Those smells were quite real, and stung my eyes as well as my nostrils. However, the conversation I had followed was not.

I had been taken in by a skillful illusion. And only confronting an inconsistency in the illusion — that I heard the sound of conversation and yet could see no source where a source had to be — allowed me to break through the confines of said illusion enough for my senses to warn me of danger.

My neck ruffled. My solar plexus trembled.

The sounds of conversation stopped entirely.

I turned to escape. Five green pentacles flared to life at key spots on the dirty concrete floor.

The circle was closed, and I was trapped as neatly as any demon.

Of course, I doubted at first. They might have erred in casting their circle.

I tried to cross the faintly glowing green line connecting the inverted pentacles. I could not.

*"How could not?"* Harley asked. *"Like trying to put your foot through a wall?"*

Not in the least. There was no barrier perceptible to my senses. It was simply that, in attempting to cross that barrier with my feet, my hands, or even my head, as I reached the barrier I simply ... went no further.

It did not physically repel me, and yet no amount of effort would carry me across.

*"I assume you tried closing your eyes, and tricks like that?"* Sebastian *asked, in his nigh-infinite arrogance.*

You may presume I attempted all of the simple tricks that might have allowed me to cross an imperfect circle. Not one of them worked, or there would be no reason to bother the three of you with this story.

*"Of course," Sebastian said, not sounding the least contrite.*

*"Pabst Blue Ribbon," Clark said, bringing Zed his beer. "Food'll be just another few minutes."*

*Clark was intelligent enough not to linger.*

*"The boxes," Zed said, when Clark was once more behind the bar. "One of the pentacles had to be beneath them, didn't it?"*

It was. I saw that pentacle from my vantage point of trying to leave only because the bright green color stood out so strongly against the darkness behind the boxes. And no, none of the boxes crossed the line formed by the pentacles in any way that would have been useful to me.

The line, in point of fact, continued through them without difficulty, because, of course, nothing within them was constrained by the circle in the way that I was.

Now. If I might continue *without interruption?*

Once I tested the boundaries of the circle physically, I had to test them magically.

I retreated to the center of the circle. And if any of you pretend to lack the knowledge that the center if the place of strongest power within any cast circle, I shall cease wasting *my* time in telling you all this story.

Thank you.

I scuffed the spot as clean as I could make it, using only the soles of my shoes. I then sat in the half-lotus position, so that I might sink myself into a light trance state and project my consciousness from within the confines of my body.

Alas, my astral form found the borders of the circle as impenetrable as my physical form. I had suspected it would, but proper troubleshooting technique required me to eliminate all obvious possibilities first.

With the more precise magical vision afforded to me by working directly from the astral, I could see that the circle had, in fact, been inlaid within the concrete, using a ring of gold. It had then been covered over with a light, though recent layer of concrete.

The ring of gold appeared to be thin, and poured directly into a groove inlaid in the concrete. However, even a thin ring of such size — approximately fifteen feet in diameter — required enough gold to represent a not inconsiderable expense.

An expense given a higher priority than completion of the house itself.

Therefore, the owner had always intended to use this space for magic. Further, the proper inversion of the pentacles suggested that the owner's path might be congruent with my own.

I returned to my body. Stood. Dusted myself off.

I approached the only exit with my shoulders back and my head held high.

I reached toward the edge of the circle. But not merely with my hand outstretched. I formed the horns of He Whom We Follow and muttered softly those passphrases taught to me following the highest of my initiations.

None of the passphrases served me. The circle would not release me.

And worse than that, the circle and pentacles flared brighter. As though whoever had cast the circle had prepared it to defend against one such as I.

This was no mere a trap lain for any passerby who happened to become curious about the odor of ammonia.

This was a trap set for me.

---

ANGER IS A USEFUL TOOL, IN THE HANDS OF ONE TRAINED IN ITS applications. And anger, I had in abundance. One might even feel inclined to label my state of mind as "rage."

I, myself, would dispute that categorization as implying a lack of control. While I, even then, felt most decidedly *in* control of myself.

Though I do confess, the depth and heat of anger *connotated* by the word "rage" certainly fit my state of mind as comprehension dawned regarding the truth of my confinement.

My fury so reddened my vision that the green of the pentacles seemed almost brown for a moment.

The sting of the ammonia, so thick in the air, lent both fuel to my fire and coherence to my thoughts.

Perhaps they knew I was coming. But they could not know exactly when, nor what I would do once trapped within their circle.

What was more, they were clearly running an actual methamphetamine laboratory here. Which meant that they might have accidentally left something nearby that could assist me.

I glanced over the beakers and Bunsen burners. Nothing useful there. I knew that such labs as this one were prone to unfortunate explosions and fires, but neither would serve my purposes.

I could burn down the structure around me. But if I did not first find a way to break the circle, I would die trapped within it.

*"But fire—" Sebastian started, though I did not bother waiting for the rest of his sentence.*

Of course I could keep the flames themselves away from my person. However, once the structure above me began to collapse, even I could not guarantee myself a safe place to stand.

Could any of you?

*Harley looked for a moment as though he might suggest that he could. Interesting. However, he sipped from his beer instead of speaking up.*

No?

Then please allow me to continue.

I turned off the heat under the beakers, then disconnected their propane tank. That did little to abate the ammonia smell, alas, but it did reduce the propane noise. Now, on this side of the makeshift corridor, I had only the one, small propane tank feeding the camp lantern.

I checked the stack of cardboard banker boxes. Alas, they were largely empty, save for a handful of empty plastic bags, three black markers and … one full box of product. Perhaps five kilograms of crystalized methamphetamine, stored within a single, large plastic baggie.

The crystals looked clear, and bluish. Likely high quality. Even my inexpert eye could tell that this had to be worth a great deal of money.

This had possibilities.

*"Wait," Sebastian said, once more testing my patience with a question. "'Inexpert eye?'"*

Are the words unfamiliar to you, Sebastian?

*"Of course not. But if you know so little about crystal meth, what did you want with the lab in the first place?"*

As there seems to be some confusion, let me first make clear that it is my considered opinion that those who have addicted themselves to drugs — leaving aside as another category that minority who have been addicted by others — represent the weak and disorganized of mind.

*"That's hardly fair," Sebastian said. And I believe he would have said more, had I let him.*

Do you wish to debate the nature of drug addiction? Or do you wish to hear why I investigated the laboratory in the first place?

Thank you.

Now. To continue. Those who act as middlemen, retailers of the end product, are often little better. In general, neither the users nor the middlemen tend to be worth my time.

However, those who *produce* the product, I find, tend to have stronger, more organized minds — which means that they have potential — while still falling into two categories.

The ambitious and the desperate.

I can offer a great deal to the ambitious and the desperate. And when the ambitious and the desperate have potential, I can gain a great deal myself in the bargain.

That, my friends, is why I followed the stench of ammonia down into the basement that day.

Now, then.

I considered returning to the center of the circle and seeing what forces I could bring to bear against the wards that contained me.

I quickly discarded that option as useless. If this trap were set for me, as it seemed to be, then there was no point in wasting my resources. Those who laid this trap were clearly organized enough to be taken seriously, which implied that they would be as prepared for me to try to break this circle, magically, as I would be for any demon summoned and constrained within a circle of my will.

Or, at the very least, that was the safest working presumption. I could not afford to underestimate my captors.

Ergo, I had only my finest tool available to me: my mind.

And as I could find within the circle nothing that would aid me directly, I would have to seek aid from without the circle.

After all, those who trapped me had to want something.

I took a moment to draw a useful circle, surrounded by the right symbols, in the center of the concrete. Just in case circumstances shifted and I required it quickly.

I then went back to the part of the circle closest to the opening into the makeshift corridor.

"Very well," I said in strong, carrying tones. "I am here. Where, apparently, you want me. Which means that some one of you must be nearby for this eventuality. Otherwise you risk my escaping without your profiting in the least."

"You couldn't possibly escape, Eamon," a deep voice said. The deep voice was accompanied by an arrogant smile. And the arrogant smile sat in the smarmy face of a tall, blonde man who clearly spent too much time in the gymnasium and too little time in the library.

Even a rank apprentice should know better than to taunt a trapped demon. Because no matter how the scenario resolves, that demon will not spend all eternity within that circle.

And my thirst for vengeance is as strong as any demon's.

"That's right," he said, finishing what I assume was a thought. "We know who you are."

I looked him up and down, as though uncertain about him. I noted that under his white tee shirt he had a number of tattoos, but couldn't tell what they depicted. He wore cut-off jean shorts, and sneakers older than any article of clothing I owned.

His skin was bare of hair. Not just a clean-shaven chin, but his legs and forearms as well. This suggested that he was a swimmer, or bodybuilder.

He carried too much bulk for a swimmer, but not enough for a competition bodybuilder. Could be a simple case of narcissism.

Either way, he radiated thug. Not at all what I initially expected, but I could see the logic of it. He was kept for his looks, not his brains.

I could exploit that. If I could do so before the real threat showed up.

"So you aren't the one who cast the circle," I said, not even pretending it was a question. I frowned. "Surely they could not have left a dullard like *you* to negotiate." I leaned forward a little. "Is your mommy or daddy home?"

He gnashed his teeth at me, and pulled back both fists as though he were fool enough to strike me.

I pushed him. Looked him right in the eye and laughed.

"Aww," I said, in my most acerbic tones. "Is 'ums cwoss? Did bad old Eamon point out that you're stupid?"

He growled, as though the full moon were about to break through the clouds and turn him into a werewolf.

But there was no moon. It was still early morning. And he was no werewolf.

He took a step closer. "I'm warning you."

He had a good voice for lines like that. Pity. It was wasted on him.

"Please," I said, preparing a defense, just in case. I also had to dumb down my retorts, to make sure he understood them. "I could wipe the floor with you and still have enough energy to run a marathon."

A step closer. Only one step more and he'd break the barrier.

One more step, and I was free.

"I could dismantle you and sell you for parts," he said.

"That's not bad," I said with an appreciative nod. "Who'd you steal it from? Because you're obviously too much of a colossal idiot to come up with that on your own."

He lifted his foot to take that last step.

"Dis-mant-le," I said. "Why, that's three syllables. Two more than anything in *your* vocabulary. Do you even know what it means?"

I raised me right hand, spell ready to put him down.

"Klaus!" a sharp, female voice barked. "Back away from him right now."

The real threat had arrived.

---

His mistress' voice cut him like a whip. Emotionally, at least. I saw no signs of physical damage. And yet, the moment Klaus heard his name spoken by his mistress in such sharp tones, he winced like a dog that had been beaten too many times.

*"You don't—" Sebastian began, but once more I didn't bother letting him finish.*

Of course I do not abuse dogs. Nor cats. Nor any other animals that are kept as pets in this country.

But I know an abused animal when I see one, and I was looking at one in Klaus.

His mistress had not yet said anything beyond telling him to get away from me. And yet he whirled mid-step, fell to his bare knees on the dirty concrete, and frothed with desperate apologies. His clasped hands, high and pleading.

Frankly, I found the display so distasteful that the sight of it warred with the ammonia as to which was leaving a worse taste in my mouth.

I could not yet see Klaus' mistress, though I could hear the clicking of her approaching high heels. An interesting choice of footwear, considering the terrain.

The high heels stopped. The apologies continued.

"Silence," she said, and Klaus stopped talking midsentence. "How can anything so beautiful be so useless?"

"I... I..." Klaus stuttered.

I heard the sharp report as she backhanded him across the face, knocking him to the floor.

"Thank you, mistress," he whimpered.

She stepped on his sternum with one black stiletto heel as she passed him. He moaned, but not as though in pain.

She finally stepped into full view, framed by the entryway of the makeshift corridor.

I recognized her at once, of course. The long, honey blonde hair, as well as the lithe build gave her away.

She was the woman I'd seen wearing the revealing nightgown and crossing a bedroom. Apparently she'd taken more notice from the cawing of crows than I'd realized.

She was dressed now in leather pants that became mostly straps once they passed her knees. Her top appeared to be black latex, and though it covered her from wrist to collarbone, it did less to conceal her contours than her even nightgown had.

I do confess, she was pleasant to look upon.

"Nice outfit," I said. "Though I prefer the sight of you in your nightgown. Less aggressive."

That put an arrogant smile on her face that mirrored the one I'd gotten earlier from Klaus.

"Not man enough to handle an aggressive woman?"

"Man enough to know my preferences," I said. "But I doubt you trapped me here as a prelude to seduction."

She smiled, and there was a touch of lechery to the smile. As though not yet acceding to what I considered obvious.

"Well," I said, pretending to play along. "If that's what you have in mind, shouldn't we be on the same side of the circle?"

Klaus rolled to his knees, looking at his mistress as though betrayed.

"But Mary..." he started.

She grimaced and backhanded him again.

"You will speak when you are told to speak," Mary said. "Not before."

"Mary," I said, smiling. Drawing her name out a little as I said it again.

She flared her nostrils in a show of silent irritation. It wasn't her full name. But whether she was named Mary at birth, or selected that name as a profanity to lend power to her magic, it was a name that meant something to her.

Which meant it represented power I could exploit. Perhaps not immediately, in terms of magic — given my rather restricted resources, at the time — but magic was not the only tool in my toolbox.

"Are you quite contrary?" I asked, teasing. "Shall I ask how your garden—"

"You'll be compost in my garden to help it grow," she said darkly, "if you keep that up."

"Some consider gentle teasing part of any good seduction."

"Only if the teasing has appeal to both parties. That nursery rhyme does not."

Now, realize, she described herself as "aggressive." But she understated the case. I had already determined that this was a woman who didn't just play dominance games with her lovers. This was a woman who lacked some degree of confidence within, and so attempted to spackle over the obvious gap with shows of power.

That represented a weakness of mind, and an advantage for me.

"If you would prefer," I said, "I could ask about your little lamb. Or—"

"Enough!" she barked, clapping her hands sharply.

From his place on his knees, Klaus smirked up at me. Apparently even Klaus had finally realized that Mary had no designs on my body.

Well, no sexual interest in my body, I should say. At that time, for all I knew, she intended to put my body to other uses. Human sacrifice certainly seemed like a possibility.

"So you have gotten this inept fool" — she spared Klaus a casual kick across the jaw — "to tell you that I am called Mary. And I, in the heat of the moment, tipped the truth of that. Well done."

I chose not to taunt her with a bow. I had the feeling she was leading to something.

"But is that name enough to aid you here and now?" She tapped her chin. "I wonder. What do you think?"

I held my silence, preferring to roll my wrist in a move-it-along gesture.

"I, on the other hand," she said, "know a great deal about you, Eamon Bradford."

She then went on and listed my street address, three of my more important email addresses, the numbers of four of my bank accounts, and was starting in on more when I spoke up.

"Yes, yes," I said impatiently. "I'm sure you're more than capable of paying for a half-decent private investigator's time. Even if you're incapable of finishing this house."

She laughed. Not a vicious, menacing laugh, either. She laughed as though I'd caught her off-guard with something actually amusing.

"Is that what you think?"

"Well," I said, frowning as I considered. "Assuming you *have* the money, the number of reasons to keep the house in this state are few..."

She actually let me think about it for a moment. Studied me as I did.

"It's an eyesore," I said. "From the lawn to the roof." I chuckled. "Either you or your coven, or both, want to buy more property nearby, and you think this house, in its current shape, will hurt the property values and discourage other potential buyers."

"Works, too," she said with a smile. "They took down their sign, but they're still fielding offers. Or should I say *offer*, for the others have been pulled."

"Not bad," I admitted. "But on its own, the house wouldn't do all that. Not in this market. Which demon is helping you? Kune?"

"How did you guess?" she asked, shocked.

"Well, I confess I don't recall the exact phrasing of Kune's description in the *Sworn Grimoire of Count Alfonso*, I do remember getting the impression that Count Alfonso credited Kune with the size and quality of his county. Made me think of him as good for real estate matters."

"Alfonso started life as a landless serf," Mary said. "Was drafted into war, acquitted himself well and knighted on the battlefield. But he was a landless knight until Kune began working with him."

Mary nodded. "That was well reasoned. Pity."

"Pity what?"

"Well, under other circumstances, I think we might have worked together well." She shrugged, and I taunted her by ignoring her torso as she did. "But it's not to be."

"So you mean you're really not here to seduce me?" I asked in a flat tone.

"Of course not," she said with a smile. "And not everything I know about you came courtesy of a private eye."

She named my coven. A name she could not have gotten from any private eye.

Hearing that name from her lips did more to accelerate my heartrate than attending a skyclad ritual would, even if it was performed entirely by supermodels.

But I did my best to keep my expression steady in the immediate, and followed that with a laugh that I hoped sounded natural.

"Not. Even. Close," I said, shaking my head. "Whoever your sources are, destroy them."

She smiled again. And this time, it was the smile of a sadist, confident in the pains she is about to inflict.

"A fine performance," she said, and gave me a golf clap. "But I know the truth."

"You know a lie," I claimed, shaking my head sadly.

"You," she said, ignoring my last statement, "are my key to breaking that coven. You are going to provide me all your passphrases. You are going to detail for me your defenses. And since you possess such a dizzying intellect, you are also going to provide me with the *lapses* in those defenses that you, yourself, have noticed."

"Since I cannot give you information I do not possess," I said, fighting to not to show my nervousness, "I trust you will not be offended if I ask, or what?"

"'Or what,' you ask?" she said, and her smile widened. "Or what," she repeated, as though considering the question. "Dear me. What-ever shall I do if you refuse to freely give me what I want?

"Why," she said simply, "I'll simply *have* to punish you."

She held out one hand.

"Klaus," she said, "fetch my blasting rod."

Now, as I believe that at least two of you possess no training at all in western ceremonial magic, allow me to explain.

A blasting rod is a tool used for compelling demons to obedience. It is described in *The Grand Grimoire* as carved from "a rod of wild hazel, which has never borne fruit."

Properly made, it is said to be a weapon capable of visiting great, painful tortures upon its target.

Of course, *The Grand Grimoire* also claims that the blasting rod was the weapon with which the Great Betrayer armed his angels, when they were to cast the "rebellious angels" out of "heaven."

As you might suspect, it is not a tool I myself use. Nor does any member of my coven. The associations are not ... salutary.

Also, unless one's target is currently constrained within a circle of one's will, the blasting rod is no more useful than any other branch of wild hazel.

When Klaus returned from the area on the other side of the makeshift corridor, he was carrying a three-foot rod that did indeed appear to have been cut from wild hazel, and shaped to suit its task. Sanded down well, stained to bring out the character of the wood, and engraved with what I had to assume were the proper engravings.

Klaus certainly held the rod as though it were a holy object, upraised on both his palms, with his head bowed respectfully.

Then again, I could only find that so impressive. The man was so obsequious where Mary was concerned that he likely presented her lunch in the same pose.

Mary picked up the rod with a delicate touch. With her free hand, she played fingers along its length.

"Are we back to teasing?" I asked. "Am I supposed to find that erotic?"

"Depends," she said, tilting her head so that her long hair draped down her arm. "Do you find pain erotic?"

"I am not a member of the coven you named," I lied. "I do not possess the information you desire. Torturing me would accomplish nothing."

"Next you will pretend you are entirely without magic. Even though my circle holds you."

"I do not pretend ignorance in the *ars magica*. However. I could be a newborn babe and this circle would still hold me," I said. "You targeted me specifically. Not just the first member of ... what was that coven's name again?"

"Cute," she said, and raised the blasting rod. "Now. The first outer circle password, if you please. Klaus, prepare to take notes."

"You trust that imbecile to..."

I trailed off because Klaus rapidly produced a notepad and pen, and achieved a look of intense concentration beyond anything I'd thought him capable of.

"Not so good at thinking on his feet, I'll grant you," Mary said, and favored Klaus with a smile that practically made him float with little cartoon hearts popping around his head. "But his note taking is exceptional."

"All right," I said. "That's enough of this nonsense. I've played along as far as I'm going to."

"So you'll tell me what I want to know?" Mary said, with a smile for me too. "Wonderful. Betraying such as those you've worked with is no stain on you. We might even be able to—"

She finally realized that I'd walked away from her and was fiddling with the large tank of propane, connecting it to one of the Bunsen burners.

"What are you doing?"

I ignored her, and dragged the table noisily to her side of the room. I got the fire going perhaps five feet from her. Then I placed a beaker above the flame.

"Surely you aren't fool enough to blow the place up."

I continued ignoring her. I carried the camp lantern over by the banker boxes and set it on the floor beside them. I dug through the right banker box and picked up her plastic bag full of product.

She couldn't see me where I stood. Not unless she leaned in and risked breaking the circle, which I knew she would not do.

I considered rummaging around to make her nervous, but didn't want to push her into using that blasting rod. Curiosity had stayed her hand so far.

I came back to the table, bag in hand and smile on my face.

"Klaus," Mary said sharply. "Why is that bag still in my circle?"

"Joey was late with his pickup today. Said he'd come by this afternoon."

"And you didn't move it when you heard the crows because…"

"The crows! Right. Uh…"

"Never mind," she said, shaking her head. To me she extended one hand, short of breaking the circle, and said, "Toss me the bag."

"Hate to see it spill on the dirty concrete," I said. "I'll hand it to you."

The bag of product, on its own, could not affect the circle. But if she and I were both touching the bag — passing it from within the circle to without it — *that* would break the magic of the circle.

"Toss it," she said, holding up the blasting rod again. "Or else."

I held the bag over the heated beaker, ready to pour.

"Hey," I said. "If I'm going to die today, maybe I should die smiling."

"You wouldn't," she said, actual disbelief in her voice. "You're too tightly wound to take drugs. Even at risk of your own life."

"I have nothing left to lose. You're going to kill me."

"Now hold on," she said, raising her free hand in a conciliatory gesture. "There's no reason you have to die today."

"Yes, there is," I said simply. "I don't have the information you want. So I can't give it to you. But you won't believe me. Which means you'll torture me to death, trying to get to a truth I don't possess."

"Why do you persist in this lie?"

I made a show of sighing and shrugging, as though sad that I couldn't convince her of an obvious truth.

Inwardly I smiled. I knew they weren't just worried about their product. If I dumped that much methamphetamine into the beaker, I would not be the only one affected by the smoke.

It would reach them next. And their teeth were too clean and strong to be the sort who used methamphetamine.

Also, I doubted that their illusions were ready to contain methamphetamine smoke. It would leak out. Neighbors would call the emergency number.

Mary's whole little business would be ruined.

"Enough," she said. "Toss me the bag. Last warning."

"You let me out. Last warning."

She used the blasting rod.

How do I describe pain that all-consuming?

I felt...

The closest image I can think of is this.

I felt as though each and every nerve ending in my body were being sandblasted by the entire Sahara Desert.

When next I had awareness of anything else, I found myself lying on the concrete floor. Drooling. Shaking. Drenched in sweat and urine. Likely I would have evacuated my bowels, as well, had I not done so before leaving the house.

My heart beat so frantically I could hardly tell where one beat ended and the next began.

Somewhere nearby I could hear someone screaming ... something. Orders, perhaps. Their words made no sense. I was separated from them by a layer of cotton.

I could see two figures moving nearby. Just the other side of the smoke.

The smoke. Something on the table was smoking.

The beaker was smoking. Smoke came out of the beaker. The beaker. It was full of pretty crystals with a layer of liquid at the bottom. More crystals lay scattered across the table and floor nearby.

Something about those crystals. That smoke.

The smoke hadn't reached me yet. But it was coming. And I had to do something before it did.

What did I have to do?

Oh, yes.

By a sheer act of will, I dragged my prone body over to the circle I'd drawn in black marker.

Once inside the circle, I spat on my hand — took me three tries to get enough saliva — and touched the circle while forcing the right words out from between uncooperative lips.

My circle flared to life, red power coruscating over black lines.

The smoke could not reach me now, so long as I stayed in the circle. I'd included methamphetamine smoke as one of those things barred from entry.

I was safe from the smoke. Mary and Klaus were not.

---

RECOVERY FROM THE EFFECTS OF THE BLASTING ROD WAS BOTH QUICK and very, very slow.

It was quick in the sense that I regained my faculties rather rapidly, and was able to think and act without losing too much time.

It was very, very slow in the sense that I can still feel it sometimes. An echo of that pain dancing along my nerves like an aftershock of nightmare.

Mary was shouting and trying to hit me with her blasting rod again and again.

Her blasts no longer harmed me.

Now, I would like to credit my immunity to further strikes to my own magical creativity. But in truth, there are two possible reasons why her further applications of the blasting rod failed to harm me.

The first was that, by casting my own circle within hers, I had created a safe zone for myself. A place where I was confined by my own will, not constrained by hers. And thus, an ineligible target for her blasting rod.

I favor that possibility, of course, because I find it elegant and flattering. However, I cannot say, with certainty, that this was the reason for my safety.

The second possibility was that her focus may have been off. Either worried about, or already feeling the initial effects of, the methamphetamine smoke.

The blasting rod was still a tool of will, and if her will was divided, she may have failed to work that tool correctly.

Either way, I had a moment to gather myself.

I drew myself into a crouch as though waiting for a starter's pistol. Mary and Klaus could not afford to let too much more of their product burn, or the spread of smoke would bring their operation up in flames.

Mary finally cracked and screamed, "Klaus!" She lowered herself into a guard position. Ready to oppose me when I came her direction.

Klaus darted across the circle.

The green fire of the pentacles around me extinguished at once.

I bolted for the place where the makeshift corridor began, nearest to the stairs and freedom.

Now, I realize that I do not look imposing. But I maintain a solid regimen of diet and exercise. I had not Klaus' muscles, but I do not lack strength.

Furthermore, I have the intelligence to note a weak spot in a shabby nail job.

I hit the curtain of floorboard that had been hung like a wall. Right at it's weakest spot — beside the stairs.

I popped enough of the nails out to get myself through, and hit the stairs running.

I heard more screaming behind me, but paid it no mind.

The blasting rod might have done me real damage on a spiritual level — I may be recovering from that one strike for months — but it also awoke my adrenaline glands with a vengeance.

I ran all the way home at double my normal pace, and did not slow until I was safely inside my own wards once more.

5
___

# CLARK

WHEN EAMON FINISHED TALKING, THE BAR WAS SO STILL THAT I JUMPED when the AC kicked on. I was standing behind the bar at the time, warring internally between interrupting his story and letting their food get cold.

"All right," I said, forcing joviality into my voice and bringing over their tray of food.

They looked up at me as though they'd forgotten I was even in the same city, let alone the same building.

For just a moment, every one of them — and yes, I'm including Sebastian in this — gave me a look so cold I started shaking.

I realized in that moment that every one of those men could kill me without a moment's hesitation, and that the inconvenience of losing access to my bar would bother them more than taking my life.

These men. All four of them. The looks they were giving me convinced me that they'd killed before. And would again.

That eternal moment passed as I took my next step.

Harley turned his attention to his beer. Zed, as though following his lead, did the same. Eamon shifted his eyes from mine to his jalapeño poppers, then nodded. As though only just remembering he'd ordered them.

Sebastian gave me one of his suggestive smiles, and even as I was telling myself that he couldn't set me at ease again. Not after what I'd just seen, and what I'd been hearing. Even as I was telling myself those things, I could feel my muscles relaxing and my smile growing more natural.

And that disturbed me even more than the looks the gruesome foursome had given me only seconds before.

"Okay," I said. "Fried tentacles for Harley, poppers for the table, and two brownies for Sebastian, with one big scoop of vanilla ice cream drenched in hot chocolate, and topped with a maraschino cherry."

Once I'd distributed the food, I tilted the tray up like a shield protecting my chest, and said, "Anyone need fresh drinks?"

Eamon circled one finger and pointed at his glass. Harley nodded at his two-thirds empty glass.

"Still working on my daiquiri," Sebastian said, as though apologizing for having a glass still half-full.

Zed merely shook his head once.

"Back with them shortly."

Once I was back behind the bar, Harley broke the silence.

"So, not Carters then."

"Obviously," Eamon said. "But trouble enough all the same. I've been digging around about them. Calling up the usual demons and servitors."

"With the aid of your coven?" Zed asked.

"Haven't told them yet," Eamon said with a shake of his head.

"Of course," Zed said, which made me wonder why he'd asked the question. "Better to go to them with a victory than a defeat."

"What have you found out?" Sebastian asked.

"I'll save that for now," Eamon replied. "Until we know whether we're all helping each other with our recent difficulties."

"Never did say what your primary hubris was," Harley said.

"That's not all," Sebastian said. "Didn't tell us why it was so important that you start your story where you did, instead of starting at your discovery of the meth lab."

"I should have thought both were obvious," Eamon said with a smug smile. "Their answers are the same, after all. My primary hubris was that I'd allowed myself to fall into the same exercise pattern, where my daily run was concerned. Which was why I had to start the story with just that pattern."

Eamon shook his head. "I rose at the same time every day. Left my house at the same interval, jogging in the same general area." He grimaced. "I might as well have put a target in the center of my back and left the house chanting 'shoot me, shoot me' as I ran."

"Exaggeration," Zed said. "Obviously they were not ready when you arrived. They relied on warning systems. And even so, Klaus committed key errors, leaving both the bag of product and black markers available for your use."

"They couldn't know what day I'd arrive," Eamon said, "or what hour. Not without using a magical lure that would risk alerting me."

"They didn't have to," Sebastian said. "That's the point. They simply laid their snare along a path you'd cross eventually."

"Hunters lay more than one snare," Harley said, pointing at Eamon with his beer.

"True," Eamon said, "but in this case I doubt they've gone to that much effort. That location is important to Mary and her coven for other reasons. Therefore they laid the trap knowing I'd run that direction at some point, and they wanted to catch me when I did. Rather than risk my catching them unawares and getting the first move."

Eamon sighed. "The predictability of my morning routine made me ripe for just such a trap, while requiring minimal effort on their part."

I had to bring the drinks back at this point, but didn't want to interrupt them long enough to clear any empties. I just distributed the beers, hurried back behind the bar, got out last night's receipts, and pretended to review them.

Just as I did, Sebastian spoke up.

"All right, gentlemen. I'm next."

## 6

## SEBASTIAN

Mmmm.

Much of my week was as sinfully delightful as I could make it. All the way through Saturday night.

Ah, Saturday night. You know, once the alcohol starts flowing at a college party, the line between "raging kegger" and "frenzied orgy" grows thin. And easing the hesitant across that line is oh, so easy…

*"Sebastian," Eamon objected.*

*"Gotta agree with Eamon here," Harley said. "Coming mighty close to proselytizing again."*

*"And even if not," Zed added, "even you must admit that this hardly describes the beginning of a problem."*

*"More like a letter to* Penthouse," *Harley muttered.*

Now, now. Don't mean to make ya'll jealous. I'll tone back the details to levels that wouldn't even make a porn star blush.

All right. All right. Don't overexcite yourselves. I'll just get on with it, and leave the night before to your imaginations.

More's the pity.

Point is, everything seemed to moving along well through Saturday night. To the degree that I was able to offer up amazing amounts of passion to the Wild One while having myself a good old time in the process.

I fully expected to awaken that next afternoon naked and covered in barely legal teenage flesh.

Problem was, I did nothing of the sort.

I did wake up. That much went right.

However.

I woke up sometime that *morning,* not afternoon. After having fallen asleep somewhere around the time that our Spartan friend here was waking up. So I got a couple of hours heavy sleep at the most.

Not nearly as much as I needed after a night like Saturday night.

And I did not wake up in a big, comfortable bed, covered in bare, luscious teenage flesh, with a sumptuous breakfast waiting for me when I finally left that bed.

I woke up, rather, in a field of dry, yellow grass.

*"Where is there dry, yellow grass around Portland this time of year?" Eamon asked.*

One of the first fifteen questions I asked myself. But let me finish setting the scene.

I was not gloriously naked, as I expected to be, but wearing loose, white linen pants tied at my waist with a drawstring. I wore a similar shirt — white linen — done in a simple tee style, with a V-neck that at least gapped low enough to imply good things about my chest. Though really, the fit was atrocious.

In fact, both the pants and shirt were cut too big for me. They hung as though I were a famine victim.

The sandals on my feet fit better, at least. Though the leather was cheap enough that I worried I'd get a rash. And the soles and ties were so worn I couldn't doubt that the sandals were used.

As I tend to run a little hot, cold rarely bothers me. So the chill of the morning air was nothing. But I'd had so little sleep that the sun seemed painfully bright.

*"Too little sleep?" Eamon tried to taunt me. "Or too much alcohol?"*

Now, none of you can cry *proselytizer* if I answer a question. So let me just say that if I still had to suffer the consequences of my drinking, while participating in the rites and celebrations of my sect, I'd hardly be qualified to sit at this table, now would I?

However. I don't think it's telling tales out of school to admit that sleep is important for me. And waking up the way I was, well, that it left my resources somewhat depleted.

So I was not exactly at my best as I tried to figure out just where I was and just what had happened to me.

I got to my feet and looked about. This wasn't just some field of wild grass, as I'd originally thought. It was a recently harvested field of hay. I could still see rolled bales from where I stood. Maybe six of them. None less than maybe eighty yards away.

*"Not at your best?" Zed asked.*

I didn't determine all this in the span of a few seconds. I had to shield my eyes, grit my teeth and look around, counting out loud. Must I admit to every limitation?

*"If we're going to help," Harley said, "you can't just paint a rosy picture of yourself."*

All right. All right. I shall confess the litany of my shames.

My empty stomach growled. Because I was hungry, obviously, but also because I was smelling the sweet fragrance of freshly harvested hay.

Whoever had dressed me up and carted me out here did so without leaving even a continental breakfast for me.

Thoughts of food made me realize that my mouth was dry.

*"Of course your mouth was dry," Eamon said. "Between the drinking and—"*

For a man who claims to have such an organized mind, your memory seems to be slipping, Eamon. Didn't I just tell you that I do not suffer the downsides of alcohol the way others do?

I had every reason to expect to wake up that morning with my mind free and clear, my morning wood hard and ready, and my breath fresh and clean.

And yet, I was groggy. My mouth was dry. And what hung between my legs was still sleeping.

*"Without meaning to offend you,"* Zed said — *proving that I was going to have to cope with more interruptions than I offered* — *"could you have offended your patron?"*

*"A fair question,"* Eamon added. *"What you're describing could be an alcohol blackout, followed by the usual symptoms. Which, as you say, could not happen if you remained in good standing with your patron."*

Now, see, this is why I wanted to begin with the party the night before. If you all weren't such big prudes, you'd know that after what I'd done the night before, the only thing my "patron" — to use your patriarchal term, and not my own preference — would say to me is "Bravissimo! Encore! Encore!"

In short, I was definitely in the plus column, so to speak.

Now, the grogginess, that could've been lack of sleep. But Old Reliable still sleeping between my legs? And me, awakening with a dry mouth that tasted kind of like medicine?

No. Somebody drugged me.

———

STARK TERROR IS NORMALLY A SENSATION I SAVOR. EVEN WHEN IT'S MY own. Without proselytizing, I think I can admit that I like to hold the ripcord handle as late as I can, when I go skydiving.

Those extra few seconds, while the wind pounds ripples into my flesh. My heart racing, begging my arm to straighten. To pull the cord. To loose the chute that will fill with air and allow me to drift safely to the ground, rather than plummet to my doom.

Those seconds are ... divine. Life, cresting to its zenith.

*"If you feel that way,"* Eamon says, *interrupting me yet again,* *"then why don't you—"*

But even then, I do not dare death. I seek the razor's edge of pleasure. Not the risk of slashing my own veins.

The risks are those I choose. Those I control.

But to awaken in a freshly harvested hayfield? Clad in clothes I would never choose for myself, not even to infiltrate a commune with lascivious intentions?

All of that so far, well, that could have been a joke. A joke in poor taste, but still a joke. All that was missing was a rough, simple wooden cross hanging on a length of cord around my neck. Perhaps a pamphlet listing sites on a pilgrimage route.

In fact, I think I'd been looking to see if I spotted a steeple, or some other marker of rampant Christianity, when I realized that the dryness of my mouth, and its foul taste, meant that I had been drugged.

Almost more disturbing than even that thought? I'd been drugged, but woken up *early*, rather than oversleeping.

Any drug that could keep *me* comatose long enough for the change of venue and the ridiculous outfit had to be strong enough to keep me out of commission until close to sundown.

And yet though I'd clearly been drugged, I was awake. And still on the wrong side of noon.

The stark terror that accompanied these twin realizations was not one I savored. I felt less like I was surfing life's zenith than facing a wipeout.

But at least the sensation carried with it a kickstart to my system that may have helped me shake off any lingering effects of the drugs.

My heart pounded fast and furious. Adrenaline had my muscles shrieking for action. Sweat cascaded down my body in ways that probably made me look good in spite of the awful wardrobe.

After all. I look great, glistening. Not, alas, that I could afford to think of such things at the time.

I tried to look everywhere at once. Certain I was being watched. Certain I hadn't just been dumped here, but brought here for some fell purpose.

Or worse, a *righteous* purpose.

But my body was still only so awake. In whipping around to look for threats, I tripped over my own feet and fell hard on the remnants of the hay stalks.

But gods and demons alike smile on drunks and fools, of which I felt like both that morning.

I hit the ground, just as an arrow hit the ground near me. Possibly passing right through where I'd been standing.

The arrow's fletchings were white as an unfallen angel's wings. The shaft stuck out at an angle, so I quickly surmised that the archer was somewhere off to my left.

I rolled right a dozen or so revolutions. I shouldn't have been dizzy after that — *I* shouldn't have, and you'll bitch about proselytizing if I explain why — and yet as I stopped rolling the world didn't quite.

Could have been the drugs. Could have been the lack of sleep. Hard to say which.

I closed my eyes for a second and inhaled deeply through my nose. Hoping to catch a whiff of gasoline or something that might indicate civilization — and potential safety — lurking nearby.

Alas. I smelled the earthy sweetness of the dirt and hay, with an unpleasant undercurrent of fear-sweat. Anything else was too faint for me to pick up.

I twisted around, on the ground, so my head was pointing back toward the archer. I shaded my eyes against the painful brightness of the sun and risked a look.

There was a rolled hay bale maybe ... a hundred yards that direction. Had to be sheltering the archer.

All right. My clothes might've started clean and white when those — whoever they were — put them on my fantastic body. But a wash of fear-sweat had soaked them. So after the worst roll in the hay *I*, for one, have ever experienced, my clothes were now covered in dirt and hay detritus.

Pokey and uncomfortable? Yes. But a lot harder to aim at from a good hundred yards away.

Now don't get me wrong. A little sweaty rolling hadn't turned those bright whites in to proper camouflage, but I certainly presented a tougher target than I'd been a moment before.

I rubbed my hands and face in the hay-strewn dirt as well, trying to maximize the effect.

Pity the hay wasn't tall enough to cover me. But then, if it had been, I probably would've woken in a different field.

With my face still practically in the dirt — trying to keep my eyes from giving me away — I crawled first left a few paces, then back a dozen.

I was just too tired for this. Even with the adrenaline flowing like sweet wine, my muscles were already issuing complaints. The sweet burn of lactic acids. I wasn't sure I could make it all the way to one of those other hay bales. Not on my belly.

I heard the whistle this time as the arrow came down. It *thunked* into the ground back near where I'd been.

Tired or not, I crawled another few paces back and left.

I shaded my eyes again, just above the top of the hay remnants, and took a look back towards the bale I thought was sheltering my attacker.

Sure enough. I could see movement in its shadow. Not much, but enough. I could pick out the bow, too, but again, no details.

And those details could be critical. A hundred yards, that was a pretty solid distance. And I'd put at least another ... six or eight yards between me and the spot where I'd woken up.

Distance like that could almost be safe. If the bow wasn't good enough. The bow or the archer.

Yeah, that wasn't the way to bet.

"Sebastian!"

Had to be the archer shouting my name, unless there was someone else hiding in the shade of the same hay bale. I didn't recognize the voice though. Male end of the spectrum, I thought, but on the high side. A little nasal, too, but that might have been a little judgy on my part. Wasn't exactly disposed to think well of the guy, after all.

I lay there. Waiting to hear more. If the archer thought I was going to answer, though, than he was an even bigger fool than I felt like that morning.

And if this guy was a fool, I wanted to give him a chance to prove it.

I LAY THERE IN THE DIRT AND REMNANTS OF A HAYFIELD. THE MORNING sun not too hot, but still way too bright for me. My head pounded with my lack of sleep.

I was restless. My adrenals were begging me to do something. Anything. Even getting up and running for the nearest hay bale — probably a solid sixty-yard dash — sounded better to my body than lying there and waiting for the archer to either taunt me or take another shot.

But right then, my brain was still solidly in charge. And my brain knew that trying a sixty-yard dash in these used leather sandals was a recipe for disaster.

So I lay there. And I waited.

I heard the cry of a crow not too far off. No, Eamon, not a full murder. Just a single crow, cawing as it flew. And I didn't think it was an alarm of any kind either.

More important than the crow, though, I heard the distant bass rumble of a big semi truck on a freeway. Maybe a mile. Maybe two. And I was pretty sure the archer was between me and that freeway.

Not good.

Still. Freeways had offramps. Access roads. If there was a freeway a couple of miles away, there had to be a road closer than that.

No, that was by no means a certainty. But I didn't have much to go on.

"Sebastian," the voice called again. Taunting this time.

I fought the urge to crawl a few more paces. For all I knew, he'd realized what I was doing, and was looking for another ripple in the short hay, to help him spot me.

But he clearly wanted an answer. So I gave him one.

I took one fist and softly pounded the right rhythm on the dirt, while humming a few key bars and...

Well. Let's just say I was doing the right things to kick up a little of my own magic.

From all directions came the chorus of the classic Beastie Boys' track "So What'cha Want".

I cut the music before the next verse started.

The archer laughed and climbed up on top of that hay bale.

He was a big guy. Heavy. Bearded. He was wearing a brown shirt with camo pants and a matching camo baseball hat.

His bow was the scary kind. That modern, compound design. Fiberglass, with pulleys at the ends, multiple strings, and about five little curves in the shape.

Bow like that might be able to shoot as far as a thousand yards. And big as that guy was, he could probably make full use of the bow's range.

Of course, sending an arrow a thousand yards is one thing. Accurately shooting a moving target at that range was something else.

"Now that's a neat trick, Sebastian," he called out. And he must've had some voice training of some kind. Because he didn't sound like he was shouting, but his words were carrying just fine.

"You use tricks like that," he continued, "to get my Jolene to give it up?"

Okay. Disgruntled ... boyfriend, husband, brother ... maybe even father. Couldn't tell how old the guy was. Either way, the scenario seemed clear enough. I slept with this Jolene, and he was unhappy about it.

*Homicidally* unhappy about it.

Probably husband or father then.

But who was Jolene? That was the more important question, and possibly the key to my escape.

*"All right," Eamon said. "Don't you dare try to tell us that you remember every bed partner you've ever had. I can't even believe you learn all their names, much less remember them."*

For a man who complains about reasonable interruptions, Eamon, you certainly provide an unreasonable share yourself.

However.

I shall answer your accusation in two parts.

First. Yes, I learn the name of everyone I have sex with, no matter what kind of sex. Even if I wordlessly meet someone in a truck stop bathroom, we lock eyes, and we do something quick and amazing together before parting in silence.

I still gain that person's name.

You have your magics. I have mine.

Second. No. I don't *actively* remember the name of everyone I've had sex with. The sheer volume of names would be unwieldy.

My sect, however, has techniques for remembering such things. And, as it turns out, I'd only had sex with one Jolene.

Clearly I haven't spent enough time in the south.

Anyway, this particular Jolene would have been six or seven months ago...

*"You remember names but not dates?"*

I swear, Eamon.

*"He's right, Eamon," Harley said. "Lay off and let the man talk."*

Thank you. Now. As I was saying. It wasn't long after the Timbers' big victory at the MLS Cup. While sports themselves have never been favorite pastimes of mine, I greatly enjoy victory celebrations.

At this particular party, I met a very pretty southern expatriate named Jolene. I'll spare you the details, but now I understood why her fiancé might be a touch peeved at me. I am, after all, a tough act to follow.

I was also pretty sure now that the archer was her fiancé. What was his name? She mentioned him at one point. Something short and harsh. Hank. Rick. Chuck. Something along those lines.

And no, Eamon, I have no tricks to help remember that name. I didn't sleep with *him*, after all.

Though I confess I was just wondering if that might be my way out of this situation when he spoke again.

"Nothing?" he called out. "No denial? Do you even remember her? Or was she just another notch on you bedpost?"

Long as he was talking, he wasn't shooting. That much was good. But his tone was getting angrier, which meant arrows were going to follow soon.

Unfortunately, I couldn't think of anything I could say that might forestall his shooting.

But was he someone who got more accurate when he got angry? Or would rage throw him off? Either way was a gamble, and I couldn't control the odds.

"What about the kid, you sleazy son of a bitch!" he hollered, and I could practically hear him frothing at the mouth now. "Yeah! That's right! Jolene's knocked up. You got a fancy fucking song for that one?"

Pregnant? Jolene was pregnant?

Oh, this just went from bad to worse. Because no way was that kid mine. And no way the archer would believe me.

## 7

---

# CLARK

The gruesome foursome grew silent as Sebastian finished his daiquiri. He started to raise his empty glass, then shook his head.

"Clark," he called, in his normal, slightly suggestive tones. As though he hadn't just been telling a tale of someone hunting him over a child that wasn't his.

I swear. I was standing there behind the bar, barely even pretending to review the receipts while Sebastian had been telling his story.

Eamon, well, he's always come across as stuck up. Smarter than thou and twice as important. But Sebastian, he'd always seemed like a nice guy. Even if he was more into sex and rich food than was probably healthy. Even knowing he was one of the gruesome foursome, it was kind of hard for me not to root for him.

Likely because, and I found myself admitting it, what with my sweaty palms, flushed face and pounding heart, I had a bit of crush on him.

Still. That story. The orgy he'd what ... caused? He could cause an orgy? Most guys, that would sound like exaggeration. Like the number of guys who claim to have had a threesome. I mean, what are the odds?

But the way he said it, and the way the others reacted. I couldn't doubt it was true.

And then he'd talked about making music out of *nothing*. To make the air itself turn a harvested hayfield into a one-song Beastie Boys concert.

No wires. No hidden speaker. Just ... magic. Real magic.

This was some spooky shit. And I didn't know how to feel about it. Except that I stood there, frozen in my pretense of looking over receipts, until Sebastian said my name not a second time, but a third.

"Clark!"

I finally looked up.

"Riveting reading?" he asked. And all four of them were staring at me now. Suspicious, maybe.

"I think the night guy was off." I shook my head and tried to sound weary instead of nervous. "Not a lot, but enough that it's a problem. I'm going to have to double-check myself though."

I wedged a smile on my face. "Can I get you something?"

"Another round for the table. But instead of the daiquiri, I'll take a black and tan."

"And more fried tentacles," Harley added. "And some onion rings, while you're at it."

"You got it, guys." I said, still with that forced smile. And I listened hard while I got their drinks and food together.

"So your birth control failed," Eamon said. "Happens. Even condoms aren't one hundred percent effective."

"You don't understand," Sebastian said, and he sounded torn between irritation and ... something else I couldn't quite put my finger on. "We have a rite. Turns off out fertility until we're ready to procreate."

"Hardly any risk in that," Zed said. "I thought risk was important to you."

"Not when it comes to this," Sebastian said with a firm shake of his head. "My sect, we consider children divine innocents. We don't harm them. We don't abuse them. We don't leave them parentless in our wake."

Sebastian's tone grew dark as he added, "In fact, my sect is more than happy to seek out and punish those who abuse children."

"Awfully noble of you," Harley said, as though he couldn't believe it.

"Nothing noble about it," Sebastian said. "Children are naturally driven by pleasure. They are sacred. Each, perfect in a way that adults inevitably lose. Even followers of the Wild One, such as myself."

"That's why you asked about pets," Eamon said, and for the first time in a while, he sounded more curious than challenging. "Pets are scared to you too."

"Divine innocents," Sebastian said with a nod. "Like children."

"All right," Eamon said, smirking now. "So you were guilty, but only partway in this case."

"So what did you do?" Harley asked.

Sebastian smiled now, and looked up at me. As though he'd somehow sensed that both drinks and food were ready. (I'd kept the deep fryer hot, just in case.)

"I waited for our drinks," he said.

I carried the tray over.

"All right," I said. "Fried tentacles, onion rings and Guinness for Harley. Pabst Blue Ribbon for Zed" — who didn't look as though he'd drunk more than a third of his second beer — "Teufelsbrau red for Eamon, and a black and tan for Sebastian."

"What did you use for the tan?"

"I mixed the Guinness with Newcastle Brown Ale."

"And that's why you're the best, Clark," Sebastian said with a smile that made me feel better despite myself. But he didn't start talking again until I was back behind the bar.

8

———

## SEBASTIAN

So there I was. Huddled and hiding in a recently harvested hayfield, while an archer with a hell of a bow accused me of knocking up his fiancée.

The nearest thing to me that was at all like cover was a big roll of hay at least sixty yards away. And running in sandals didn't sound like a great idea.

*"Why not ditch the sandals?" Zed asked, and while I didn't appreciate the interruption, I had to admit it was a reasonable question. For Zed, anyway.*

Zed, is there something about my sybaritic lifestyle that misleads you into believing I have any callouses at all on my feet? No. I assure you. If I did, they'd be buffed gently away during my weekly mani-pedi.

So running on that field in my bare feet sounded like an even worse option than the sandals.

I will say, though, that I'd now had several minutes of adrenaline pumping through my veins that morning. Which had done a good deal to shake off my grogginess. I still wouldn't be a hundred percent until I got eight or ten hours of sleep and a good meal.

Twelve. Make that twelve hours' sleep. Yeah. That sounds more right.

Point is, by now I had enough focus that I didn't feel *completely* vulnerable.

Escape, though, didn't feel like an option. Not so long as he had more ... arrows...

How many arrows could he have brought? Quivers generally didn't hold more than maybe a dozen, if I recalled right. And I wasn't sure I did. Of course, he could've been carrying more in his...

How had he gotten out here?

He had a vehicle. Had to.

And the logical place for that vehicle? Right behind the hay bale he stood on.

I had to lure him away from that hay bale.

"Come on!" the archer yelled. And now he *was* yelling. Losing some control. Good. "Face your death like a man!"

Really? I mean, of all the things he could've yelled, he went with something that played into stereotypical gender roles?

Clearly this guy had no idea who he was dealing with.

I hit him with some more music. "Billie Jean" by Michael Jackson. Not the whole song, you understand. Just the part where he denies parentage.

As the last notes echoed off, the archer screamed and loosed a shaft.

I held my breath. Afraid to move. Afraid not to.

The arrow came down less than ten yards from me.

"That's your denial?" he roared. "That's your..."

He trailed off. I risked a glance, and he was looking around. Maybe trying to figure out where the music came from.

This guy. He didn't find me on his own. And he sure didn't sneak into that party, drug me, dress me up and dump me in a field so he could play William Tell.

No. If this guy had found me naked and unconscious in a pile of college students, he likely would've woken me with a scream and then just pummeled me into new and exciting shapes.

Somebody set this scenario up for him. And that somebody, they had to be getting something out of all this too.

And right now, the archer was wondering the same thing. Wondering if maybe, this was some kind of trap for him too. Or at least, I hoped he was. Confusion to my enemy was my only real chance.

"What's going on?" he asked. Not shouting now. Speaking again, and not quite even in that carrying voice he'd been using before. In fact, if I hadn't been hoping to pick up the sound of another distant truck — and I thought I heard one, but it might've been wishful thinking — I might not have understood his words.

I gave him "I Don't Know" by Ozzy Osbourne.

"Stop it!" he hollered.

I considered taking off my shirt and waving it around as a white flag. But for one, it was pretty dirty, and for two, in his current state of mind, I was more likely to get an arrow than a parley.

But I had to do something.

I drew a deep breath and stood up. Desperately trying to call "time out" with both hands. He nocked an arrow. Pulled back to shoot.

"Damn it, hold on!" I said. "They're playing both of us!"

I emphasized the point with a chorus of "Party Time" by 45 Grave. The first time a song played that didn't match what I was saying. Had to hope that would help my cause.

*"Last time," Eamon said, interrupting for what, the fifteen millionth time? "you had to drum a rhythm with your hands and chant—"*

Yeah, but I was more together now than I had been when I started. By now I could think the tune and tap my toes, down where the archer wouldn't see the movement in the hay.

Now, if I might continue.

When "Party Time" blare out, I looked around like I didn't know where the music was coming from either.

That song cut as quickly as the others had.

"Come on," I said, and I have enough training that I can make my voice carry well too. "When the hell would *I* have had a chance to rig an audio setup? Between arrows? Think, man!"

"They said ... they said I shouldn't let you talk." He sounded hesitant now. Like maybe he was willing to listen.

I might not get a better chance.

"They're lying to you," I said. "Look. It's impossible for me to have gotten Jolene pregnant. I've been snipped. And I can prove it."

"Prove it how?"

"Get me to a computer. I'll pull up my medical record. Show you the exact date and time of the procedure, and the follow-up check on my sperm count to prove that I'm firing blanks."

Eamon, before you ask, obviously I could do no such thing. But that didn't matter, of course. If I could get him listening, I was pretty sure I could talk that guy into almost anything.

Unfortunately, in my eagerness to establish my lack of parentage, I'd overlooked a teeny, tiny little detail in my denial.

"So you admit you fucked her! You fucked my fiancée!"

Oops.

I dove left just in time. That bow could shoot an arrow pretty darned fast. I swear it practically nicked the sole of one of my sandals.

And the archer didn't stop at one. I started rolling, together enough now that dizziness was no longer a factor.

Problem was, he was tracking my movement well. The second arrow might've hit the ground behind me, but I rolled right into the shaft of the third. I snatched it, to get it out of my way, and kept rolling.

He was hollering at me now, too. Taunting me, as he took his shots. Enjoying himself. Of course, by my estimate, he'd gone through about half his quiver and had yet to draw blood. So I was coming out ahead so far.

But his shots were getting closer and closer.

OH, JUST SPIT IT OUT ALREADY, EAMON. YOU'RE GOING HAVE A conniption if you don't.

*"I just don't understand," Eamon said, shaking his head as though honestly puzzled. He might've looked cute, if he weren't Eamon. "You weren't constrained. You weren't enchanted. You'd shaken off at least most of the effects of any drugs in your system. You might not have been at your best, but surely you could have done something. You could see him. You even had a direct link in your hands. One he'd touched only seconds before — the arrow. Why didn't you hit him back? It's not as though you don't have at* least some *magical resources."*

Finished? Got all that out? Good. Wouldn't want you to choke on it.

Thank you, Eamon, by the way, for being willing to admit out loud that I can, in fact, work some magic all on my lonesome. I know those words must've tasted sour coming out. Maybe another sip of beer would help?

Maybe I could stake you to a brownie. They're pretty tasty.

No? All right then.

Now. Maybe you — maybe all three of you for that matter — go around just hexing all your adversaries into tiny little puddles of sad. But that's just not how my sect and I do things.

I'm not saying I couldn't have found some way to rain down wrath on the big guy's shaggy head. Or more likely his probably shaggy crotch. But it wouldn't have been quick, and in the condition I was in — not to mention the location, as hay fields are not especially conducive to my kind of workings, especially when they've been harvested — it wouldn't have been easy.

And if I tried, I'd make myself a big fat target while I did.

Not what I would consider a recipe for surviving to see the next sundown.

Whoever set this up, though, they'd done a pretty good job. The morning sun was off to my left. No way I could put it in the archer's eyes before he could fill me with shafts.

And I don't mean in the good way.

Pretty cloudless sky. Also to my disadvantage, for reasons that aren't worth trying to explain here and now. Let's just make clear that as metaphorical holes go, I was in pretty deep.

Almost as bad, the morning air was pretty still. Hardly any breeze so far, so even distance wouldn't be too much of an impediment to the hunter's aim.

And this guy *had* to be a hunter, the way he shot. If I were stupid enough to run straight away from him, he could probably hit me even five hundred, maybe eight hundred yards away.

Couldn't give him the chance to do that.

Hiding, though, wasn't easy. Yeah, these sweat-soaked white linens were filthy with dirt and hay detritus — which itched like a bastard, let me tell you — but he had a bead on me. Couldn't just lay in hiding the way I'd done before.

So I had to up my game.

Not just music this time.

I tucked into a backwards roll, then zig-zagged a bit to buy myself a moment.

Worked. His next shaft had to have missed me by three yards.

I might only get one chance at this, and I had to make it count. This guy was either a country fan or a heavy metal fan. At least, those were the most likely options, looking at him.

I mean, for all I knew he harbored a secret love for the stylings of Taylor Swift. But I could only go with my best guess.

*This* took a moment of stomping and chanting, while doing a couple of other key things, but I pulled it off, with the heaviest heavy metal song I could think of.

"War Ensemble" by Slayer. So loud and fast it practically seared the air.

But I wasn't just calling up music. Not this time. No, this time I gave it the rave lighting effects.

Wild blasts of vibrant, neon colors. Each a different shade of the rainbow, strobing with every beat of the drums.

And "War Ensemble" was a fast, fast song.

If this had been a darkened room, the archer would've had his mind blown. No doubt, no question. And if he had even the slightest epileptic tendencies, he'd have a seizure.

But out here in the too-bright sunshine of a spring morning? Well, the effect was less overpowering than I might've hoped.

It was all I had though. And I used that distraction to beat feet in a quick ten-yard dash off toward the archer's right, ending with a dive and a sideways roll the same direction. I held that roll as long as I dared.

I killed the music and light show the moment I stopped rolling.

I itched all over. Every quick, panting breath like stuffing dirt and hay in my nose and mouth. I was covered in fresh sweat, and half the muscles in my body were trembling. My stomach rumbled, furious that I was doing all this on too little sleep and too little food.

I shaded my eyes with a dirty hand, in hopes that they wouldn't give me away while I snuck a peek at what he was doing.

He was looking for me!

I heaved a sigh that almost made me sneeze. I had to tuck down as low as I could and clutch my nose with both hands to keep from letting that sneeze out. I know my torso convulsed a bit. I could only hope it wasn't enough to give me away.

When I risked looking again, the archer wasn't looking back at me. He was scanning the area. Watching for movement.

"Come on, Sebastian," he said. "Mustn't let 'em trick us, right? I've calmed down again. Come out and talk to me."

I didn't budge. I tried not to breathe.

"Said it yourself, Sebastian. You can't be behind the sound and light show."

Great. Something about the way he hit that "can't" told me he was lying. As though maybe he'd remembered something he'd been told by — by whoever it was who drugged me, dressed me up, and splayed me out here for target practice.

As though they'd tried to warn him about my magic, but he hadn't listened. Hadn't wanted to believe I was anything more than just another lothario, taking shameless advantage of helpless young women.

Feh. As though I'd ever once had sex with anyone who wasn't practically ripping my clothes off to get at the goods.

Compelling sex with spells is for losers.

The archer wasn't done talking though. Trying to convince me that really, we were on the same side and I should come out of hiding.

Bitch of it was, I knew I could talk my way out of this. *If* I could actually get him to listen.

But all the while, he kept that bow ready. Kept an arrow nocked. Kept his eyes scanning for the first sign of me.

That sound and light show trick wouldn't work one more time. I could tell by the way he set himself. He was ready for that.

No. If I ever wanted to see my own bed again, I was going to have to come up with something else. Soon.

---

Hunting, like seduction, largely comes down to two things: timing and patience.

Patience, because if you get in a hurry, you'll scare off your ... well, "prey" works for the hunting side, but it sounds a little rapey for the seduction side. But "intended" doesn't sound much better. Has almost a serial killer vibe.

Point is, you don't want to scare away your target, if you're hunting, or your future lover, if you're seducing. Rush and you come across as a threat.

You have to be patient. You have to enjoy the process as much as the goal.

Timing is the other key element in common to both. When your moment comes, you have to recognize it, and you have to pounce. Sometimes literally.

Now, as I lay there breathing dirt and hay, muscles twitching from bursts of speed and my head starting to ache from bright sunlight and lack of sleep, I actually had the upper hand.

Well, maybe not the *upper* hand. I mean, he was still the one with the bow and most of the arrows. I did have the one in my hand, not that it would do me much good.

Throwing that arrow would be an act of serious desperation.

But I'd worn away his patience. Gotten under his skin. That balanced things out more than a little.

Now I needed a way to throw off his timing...

Wait.

Under his skin. I'd gotten under his skin. And I had an arrow.

*"Finally," Eamon said.*

Shut up, Eamon. I told you. My sect doesn't go around hexing people, and I meant it. And I had no intention of doing anything to harm the archer.

And I didn't want the arrow to represent a missile weapon.

I closed my eyes. Cleared my thoughts, then brought my focus the right direction while humming the right tune.

I took the arrow in my left hand. Tilted it at an angle that I hoped was low enough that the archer wouldn't see what I was doing.

I sketched the archer in the dirt. Even gave him his hat, beard, and bow.

I ran the fingers of my left hand over the part of the arrow that had touched his left hand, while he aimed. I felt the connection between us, linked through this spot on his arrow.

I pulled that connection down to the left hand of my sketch.

*"With your eyes still closed?" Zed asked. "How could you be sure you were touching—"*

I was in the middle of a spell. I could've been blindfolded and spun on a centrifuge, and I'd still be able to touch any part of that sketch with perfect accuracy.

Now then. With the fingers of my right hand, I touched the part of the arrow the archer had held while pulling back his shot.

I felt the connection there as well, and pulled it down to the right hand of my sketch.

The archer to the sketch. The arrow between us. Both our hands in the same places. Touching the arrow. Touching each other.

With the connection established, I took the arrow and ... tweaked its meaning.

I jammed it down between the legs of my sketch in just the right place, at just the right angle.

Anger. Hatred. These things are powerful passions. But the bitch about passion is that it can be a fickle creature. It's the reason that some couples can't fight without fucking, and can't fuck without fighting.

Passion is the heart and soul of everything my sect does and is.

And the moment I finished my spell, lying there in that harvested hay field, that poor archer's passions got muddled.

Oh, don't get me wrong. He still hated me. But what I'd done left him also feeling stirrings and desires he'd maybe never felt before. Or at least, not for anyone he recognized as a man.

And I'd left him in, shall we say, a physical state where he couldn't pretend he wasn't feeling those desires.

*"I thought only losers seduced people with spells," Eamon said.*

This wasn't about seduction, Eamon. It was about survival. I didn't want to fuck this guy, but if I could get out of this in one piece by giving him a piece, yeah, I'd at least consider it.

*"You understand," Zed said, "that some react to such unwanted feelings with a need to kill their cause."*

Yes, but it was a risk I had to take. Not like I could be much worse off. Either way, I needed to mess with his head if I wanted to mess with his accuracy.

I took off that awful, white linen shirt now. The next time he saw me, he needed to see my muscled torso glistening with sweat.

I kept that shirt in one hand, though, in case I needed it. I considered stripping off my pants, too, but decided that a little mystery would only help my cause.

I drew one more deep breath, for courage.

I stood up and waved my shirt like a white flag.

"Can we talk?" I asked.

Just like that, he had the arrow aimed and ready to shoot.

He hesitated.

I didn't dare move.

I could feel his eyes roaming over me. His gaze taking in the muscles of my arms and torso. The length of my neck. The fall of my hair. The strength of my chin.

I swear, he almost licked his lips.

"We're both being set up here," I said. "If you think you're going to kill me and get away scot free, you won't."

He hadn't loosed that arrow yet. But damn if this guy wasn't strong. All the tension he had to be holding, and his arms were steady as a day-long rain.

"Put down the bow," I said. "Let's talk. I swear. You'll understand everything. It'll all make sense. Simple misunderstanding. You'll—"

"THEY SAID NOT TO LET YOU TALK!"

He loosed the arrow. I was so stunned I couldn't dodge.

Fortunately, either he'd been holding the shot too long, or at least some part of my spell had worked, because instead of spitting me like a pig, the arrow only grazed my left shoulder.

Still hurt like a motherfucker.

The sharp pain woke me from my daze. I dove again and started rolling and dodging while the archer screamed wordlessly and fired off shot after shot.

I didn't understand. I'd done the spell correctly. I'd felt it finish. Take hold. Yeah, I still wasn't running full steam, but I knew I had enough in the tank to at least handle twisting his passion, once I'd already gotten into his head.

Then cold realization smacked me across the face.

The people who'd arranged this. They hadn't taken any chances.

They didn't just *warn* him about my magic. They'd enchanted him themselves.

---

It's not easy to think when you're dodging a hail of arrows. And the archer was shooting just as fast as he could draw now. His screams of rage so loud, they'd echo across Oregon for a decade.

I don't know how long I kept at it. Rolling one way or the other. Scrabbling desperately on all fours to try to change his sight line.

Didn't help. His eyes were laser focused on me. But I think he was seeing as much red as anything else. Or maybe I was just that good at dodging. Couldn't really say.

No. I promised I wouldn't try to make myself look good.

I was tired and sweaty and itchy. My head was starting to ache from the brightness of the sun. Plus lack of sleep. Plus a decent amount of magic. And I was practically choking on all the dirt and hay leavings.

I swear, I can still taste hay right now, sitting here at Zoth.

Anyway, I kept moving. I didn't give up. That much I deserve. But my muscles were screaming exhaustion at me, and I was taking a lot of lumps from the ground in the process.

Oh, and getting grazed — even by an arrow — isn't one of those cool things you just ignore, like in the movies. It *hurts*. Especially if you keep moving the arm, and supporting your weight with it. Not to mention getting dirt and hay in the wound.

At least it'll heal into a pretty cool scar.

I would like to think that as I did all that dodging and rolling, I was at least leaving an artistic trail of blood behind me.

I know I left that shirt somewhere behind me. Holding onto it lost all importance in the face of a steady stream of arrows flying my direction.

On some level, I knew my ultimate goal was to try to get behind the huge, rolled hay bale that the archer stood on. My only chance of escape lay in stealing whatever vehicle he had back there.

But in the heat of the moment, all I cared about was not getting hit. There was no plan to my movements. Everything was instinct.

Duck left. Dive right. Roll. Roll. Roll.

I was stretched out and rolling lengthwise when I realized something.

No whistle of an incoming arrow. No *thunk* of it slamming into the turf. Or into my body, for that matter.

I came up to one knee. Panting like a high school boy seeing his first porno. Heart beating about that fast too. Sweat stinging my eyes and my wound.

I was about ... ninety yards from the archer. Off to his right, from where I'd started, maybe thirty degrees. Out behind his hay bale, I thought I could see the rear bumped of a huge, black, four-by-four truck...

"DAMN IT!" the archer roared bringing my attention back to him.

He was out of arrows.

I huffed a sound that might've been relieved laughter, if I had enough air.

I wasn't foolish enough to think this was over, though. And the archer proved me right.

He pulled out a hunting knife the size of my forearm. Face red and spitting fury, he roared a challenge and leaped down off the hay bale.

Had to be about a ten foot drop.

He started running before his boots hit the ground.

Mistake.

Something gave. He fell. Not on his knife. Didn't even drop it. Still, looked to hit the ground pretty hard.

I stood up. Took a moment to center myself and shake out my muscles while the archer recovered his feet. Shook away any cartoon bluebirds that might've been circling his head.

His left leg didn't want to support him. Maybe knee. Maybe ankle. Couldn't be sure which.

He howled in pain and frustration and rage and started loping after me.

Now, I bet I know what you three are thinking. Advantage, Sebastian, right? I obviously keep myself in prime physical shape. If he sprained or broke something, wouldn't be too hard for me to take advantage of the situation. Get hold of his knife. Do to him before he did unto me.

Right?

Wrong.

Truth was, I felt sorry for this guy. Not because I'd fucked his fiancée, you understand. That was just a harmless good time at a party. Not like I wanted to steal her or anything.

Plus, obviously I wasn't the only back door man in her life. Somebody'd knocked her up, and apparently it wasn't the archer.

Unless that part was a lie, start to finish. Which was a possibility, which brings us back to why I felt sorry for him.

I felt sorry for this guy because he wasn't anything more than an arrow himself.

Somebody else had set up the target. Somebody else held the bow. Somebody else had fired the shot.

Hell, even the fury that made him jump down from that hay bale was only so overpowering because my spell got mixed with his own passions and whatever magic had been done on him in advance.

Killing the archer might've ended my immediate danger. But that didn't mean he deserved to die.

I sighed, for want of running shoes.

I stood there, waiting. Watching. Gauging his speed as he approached.

When he was still a good ten yards away, I turned away and matched his speed.

This was probably going to ruin the poor guy's leg, but I couldn't help that. He was big and strong, and he hadn't been dodging and ducking from arrows on short sleep and an empty stomach.

In other words, since I wouldn't kill this guy, if he reached me I'd end up eating his knife.

And that was not an option.

So I started jogging away from him. Leading him in a big, wide circle. Hating the way my sandals slid just enough that I knew I'd get blisters. Checking over my shoulder at irregular intervals to make sure he didn't put on a burst of speed to try to catch me.

Third time I did that, I was turning my head back when I heard him moan.

Another glance. He'd waited until I finished that third check, then tried a burst of speed and failed. He'd slowed to a jagged walk, half-hopping on one foot. Hardly moving at all.

I ran flat out for his truck.

He realized what I was doing. Screamed. Probably tried to catch me. I didn't look back.

Halfway there I lost a sandal. Had to kick the other one off or lose my balance.

The rough dirt and hay played hell on my feet. But my focus was that truck.

I reached it. One of those giant Ford beasts. Dusty from the drive out here, but otherwise clean enough that the archer probably never needed the truck for its intended workhorse qualities.

He didn't lock it, either.

Oh, luxury. Leather seats. Leg and head room. Even had a back-seat. (Empty. I checked.) Felt so good to be behind the wheel and not running for my life that I sported a partial right there.

His phone was on the passenger seat, along with a piece of paper.

I locked the doors. Found his spare key on the visor. Fired up the truck with a roar — Metallica's "For Whom the Bell Tolls" was playing on his stereo — and peeled out.

I ditched the truck at the first place I could reasonably stop. A fast food parking lot. Used his phone to call ... well, let's just say I called someone who'd just love to come to my rescue when I'm half-naked and sweaty.

I factory-reset the guy's phone. Wiped it and the truck down for prints, took the piece of paper, and waited for my ride.

# CLARK

I jumped when someone banged on the back door. And I mean that literally, in both cases.

Someone knocked really loudly on the back door of Zoth. Though after listening to Sebastian spellbind me with his tale, just the phrase "back door" might never be the same for me again.

At this rate, I'd need to call Cindy after work that night, just to reaffirm for myself that I liked girls.

Anyway, I literally jumped as well. I'd been standing there behind the bar, pretending to reconcile last night's receipts. And when that pounding knock started, I jumped so hard I scattered a bunch of them.

Boy, that got my heart going, I'll tell you. And I like to think it was the sudden shock of the violent knock that had my heart racing, and not the mental image of a half-naked Sebastian, glistening with sweat.

What was wrong with me today?

When the knock came again quickly, I gave up any thoughts of grabbing those receipts. I needed to answer that door. The only people who knocked on the back door were delivery people, but I didn't have any deliveries scheduled for today.

Which made me wonder. I'd just heard two stories of parties unknown trying to kill members of the gruesome foursome. And here they all were, gathered together in one spot...

I wasn't the only one thinking this way. I could see the four of them huddled together in quiet conversation as I came out from behind the bar and stared toward the back door.

"I'm coming," I hollered as the knock came a third time. I then realized I was walking slowly, as though some hairy monster was just waiting on the other side, ready to eat me up.

I forced myself to walk normally the rest of the way.

I felt my hand hesitate as I reached for the back door, and forced myself to just open it.

No hairy monster. Well, no monster, anyway, but hairy was fair enough. It was Petey, the Guinness guy. Short and stocky enough to be a keg himself, it was as though he tried to make up in facial hair what he lacked in height.

In a past life, this guy might've been a dwarf in some fantasy world.

Speaking of kegs, Petey was in uniform, and pushing a hand truck with a keg big enough to be a third of my weekly Guinness delivery. Which came in yesterday. A fact I opened my mouth to remind him of, but I never got a word out.

"Yeah, I know, Clark," he said. Petey had the kind of voice that was higher than he liked, so he was always trying to push it down. Make it deeper.

Guy had to be pushing forty, but he still sounded like a teenager to me, playing at being an adult.

"You got your three kegs yesterday," Petey continued. "But somehow I ended up with an extra on the truck today. You want it? No charge."

This ... this just wasn't something that happened. At least not to me. I had an urge to glance over at Sebastian. Wasn't it just a little while ago that my Guinness tap had been stuck, then unjammed itself just after Sebastian ... did something? Whistled? Drew something in salt?

Was that magic? Was this?

"You sure?" I asked, as much to buy time, the way my head was reeling, as anything else. "I mean—"

"Positive," Petey said. "I take any money from you and I got to write up how I ended up with an extra keg in the first place. Which I don't know, and don't want to ask about."

"I don't want to get you in trouble, Petey," I said, frowning.

"See," Petey said with a smile. "This is why I'm offering it to you. You actually stop and worry about how this will affect me. Well, let me tell you. I haven't heard anything about a missing keg or an extra keg on the house radio all day. So they ain't missing it. Far as I'm concerned, it fell through the cracks and it's yours if you want it."

I was torn. On the one hand, I didn't want Petey to get in any trouble at all, and I thought maybe the only way that happened would be if he brought the keg back and let the warehouse guys figure out where it belonged.

Plus, if I took the keg, would I owe Sebastian for this?

On the other hand, though, my bar was never exactly rolling in money. A free bar-size keg of Guinness, that represented a boost to my cash flow that I couldn't exactly afford to ignore.

"Well, if you're sure it won't get you in trouble…"

Petey just reached up and patted my shoulder.

"Pretty quiet today, ain't it?" Petey asked as he rolled the hand truck back behind the bar to where I needed the keg.

"Always is, Wednesdays at lunchtime," I said. And just in case the gruesome foursome was listening in, I added, "Those guys do pretty well by me though."

Petey didn't care. Or at least, he didn't stay to chat. He dropped off the keg and headed back out. No doubt eager for the end of his work day. Or at least his lunch break.

Once the back door was closed behind him, I found myself frowning and looking a question at Sebastian. He merely smiled and toasted me with his beer.

His Guinness.

I turned my attention to picking up my fallen receipts.

As I did, they started talking again.

"You had his phone?" Eamon said, practically shaking with disbelief. "And you didn't dig through it? Do you have any idea how much you might've learned?"

That was his question? Not how he cracked the password and got access to the phone in the first place?

Then again, maybe that was as simple to these guys as ... producing light from nothing.

Jesus. What was I hearing? Was all this true? Could it all be an act? Maybe a live-action roleplaying group...

For a half-second, I almost convinced myself of that one.

But then I thought about that free keg of Guinness sitting behind my bar.

By the time I tuned back into their conversation, Sebastian was almost done saying something about the phone. I wasn't sure what, but he didn't sound the least bit concerned about what might or might not've been on the archer's phone.

"If he wasn't a Carter," Harley said, "he might become one now. Might not've been a bad idea, finding out more about who he is."

"If nothing else," Zed added, "he might come after you again on his own."

Sebastian sighed.

"I do wish the three of you would stop treating me like a child. My sect may not be as ... aggressive as those the three of you associate with, but I am by no means incompetent."

Eamon started to say something. Sebastian didn't let him.

"I had the man's truck, which was a marvelous link. Clearly he loves that truck and spends a good deal of time in it. And as I had time, while waiting for my ride, I made sure the archer will never find me again."

I could hear the frown in Sebastian's voice as he added, "I don't think he would've anyway. By the time I took off in his truck, I'm pretty sure he was feeling mostly shame and humiliation."

I'd found all the receipts by now — or hoped I had, because I didn't see any more on the floor around the bar — and I stood there organizing them as I continued to eavesdrop.

"What about the piece of paper?" Zed asked.

I froze. Looked for another receipt.

"Finally," Sebastian said. "I was starting to think you three weren't paying attention."

Oh. Right. His story.

Sebastian pulled out a piece of standard printer paper. Unfolded it. Showed it to the others. I could tell there was handwriting on it, and something like a big pyramid.

"The Illuminati ended decades ago," Zed said. "Pieces remain, but none use a symbol like that one."

"No," Eamon said, "but I know a group that does."

He gave the other three a significant look.

"Allied in this then?" Sebastian asked, raising his mostly empty beer.

"Allied," Eamon confirmed.

They clinked and drained their glasses.

They called for refills all around, and more fried tentacles for Harley.

And once they had them, Zed began to talk.

10

### ZED

I AND MINE DO NOT STRUCTURE AROUND PREDICTABLE EVENTS SUCH AS calendar dates or lunar cycles. Our ... larger ceremonies are based more on the ebb and flow of the zeitgeist than on anything else.

*"So you've implied before," Eamon said, "but I've never been clear. Is this a cultural zeitgeist, the broader American zeitgeist... In which sense are you using the word?"*

All and none. To us, the term zeitgeist is a shorthand way of referring to the greater essential natures of both places and people. The sense of Portland may follow the greater sense of the United States, or it may run counterpoint, depending as much on the issue as on the day.

Thus, we read, feel, and influence the zeitgeist in our minor works, to facilitate our larger works.

But we ... confine ourselves to local matters, in thought, in plan, and in action. Rarely do we stretch our reach beyond the greater Portland metro area, and never beyond the capital at Salem.

This is more indicative of our own temperaments than the needs of ... that which we serve. There are larger incarnations of our sect. We choose to remain unaffiliated with them.

*"What about Washington?" Sebastian asked, showing more insight*

*than I'd credited him with. "Vancouver is part of the Portland metro area, but the Columbia River can be a significant barrier to certain kinds of magics."*

Very good, Sebastian. In terms of zeitgeists, the pull of Washington state on its cities should not be discounted, and the barrier formed by the Columbia at Portland stands mightier — to I and mine —than the Berlin Wall once stood in Germany.

With that much made clear, it should make sense when I say that the larger ceremonies of my sect may only be performed when the zeitgeist assumes the proper shape. Either on its own — always a personal delight — or due to our own influence.

Thus, I have spent much of the last week attending meetings of the Portland City Council and certain of its committees, advisory boards, and commissions.

In truth, the week started quite well, as I believe I mentioned at our last gathering. Over the last two months, I have ferreted out the disputes and petty grievances among members of those groups wherever I could find them.

After tracking those points of contentions for the six weeks prior, and stoking them by influencing small events around the city, I was starting to see real results.

Board members breaking into loud arguments during meetings. Commissioners firing off memos so angry that word of them leaked to the press.

It was beautiful. Ripples of what I'd wrought were already showing within the zeitgeist. And I'd not yet taken the key action.

I had tensions good and seething. They needed only the right kind of match to detonate the situation into something we could use to ... use for a major working.

I planned on tossing that match at the meeting of the Portland Planning and Sustainability Commission.

The commission was set to meet on Friday at two o'clock, in one of the lesser known, or at least lesser attended, sections of city hall.

They'd moved the sessions there after last time, when a local group of homeless advocates had swarmed the meeting and carried on until the meeting had to be postponed.

Yes. The ripples were flowing through the zeitgeist, forming the loveliest pattern as circumstances came closer and closer to what I needed.

I arrived early that day. I knew security would be heightened, and they might require more than the usual screening to attend the meeting.

This would cause no problem for me, of course, but it would slow the entry process. And I wanted to be present in the room, to begin adjusting the atmosphere before the commission members themselves arrived.

This part of city hall feels constrained. The halls are a little tighter, and between the floor tiles and all the glass from the framed pictures of Portland history, echoes are tighter still.

As a child I once got to walk through mines used during the California gold rush. This part of city hall carries with it a similar feel for me. Constricting, and perhaps ready to collapse.

I moved with functional invisibility through that hall. Dressed in slacks and a button-up shirt of indistinct color and fit, I would be mistaken for a worker, a committee member, or whatever else the viewer needed to see.

I expected to pass through the police cordon unsearched, as I had done a number of times before, when meetings were considered tense enough and important enough to require a more robust police presence.

I first noticed something wrong when I reached the right hall for the meeting room. I'd turned right off the larger hall, expecting right away to find a pair of officers waiting to search visitors for contraband.

No officers stood guard. Not there at the corner, nor farther along beside the door to the meeting room.

I was thirty minutes early. Just early enough that the door should be unlocked, and any police presence should be in place and ready to perform its assigned functions.

But the police presence was a police absence. The nearest officers I could hear were dozens of feet behind me, in the main hall. Chatting with each other as they went about business unrelated to my own.

I stopped there in that side hall, just past the corner, and stretched out ahead of me with my own psychic tendrils.

City hall is usually a tumultuous mass of contrasts. Idealism and cynicism, greed and grace, plus many, many conflicting needs and viewpoints.

And most of city hall around me was just that.

But within that hall on that day, I felt quiet. An oasis of peace amid the clashes.

It was wrong. It was all wrong.

I did something then that I'm not proud of, and I have to hope no one witnessed. I hurried along the hallway. Fast enough that someone might even notice and remember me.

Fast enough that I even discovered that my not-quite-new leather shoes didn't fit as well as I'd thought, because they pinched and slid on my feet.

When I reached the meeting-room door, my worst fears had been realized.

The public meeting had been postponed.

*"That was your worst fear?"* Eamon asked in disbelief. *"That a meeting might be canceled? No. Not even canceled. Postponed?"*

Honestly, Eamon, I think Sebastian is right. You only half-listen when the rest of us are talking.

That meeting should not have been postponed. Should not have been possible. I had such anger and disagreement flowing among the members that even the *suggestion* of postponement should have brought on a near riot.

If the head of the commission were to postpone the meeting anyway, as a power play, there should have been furious commission members spouting off online, or to their local news sources. Making end moves. Using the press and the public as weapons.

Instead, there was only a sign on the door. *Today's meeting of the Portland Planning and Sustainability Commission has been postponed.*

Matters were so calm that instead of flop sweat and agitation, I smelled floor cleaner.

Floor cleaner!

Smelled like orange juice brewed in a vat of sterile perfume.

I stood there feeling the sorts of sensations I was accustomed to causing in others. Speeding heart, sweat on the forehead and under the arms, dryness of mouth. I even felt the urge to glance over my shoulder. That certainty that I was being watched.

Don't bother asking. I can practically hear all three of you wondering the same thing. No. This was not a moment of true psychic awareness of a threat. This was that sensation of the lizard brain that comes from feeling exposed and vulnerable.

And I had never felt so exposed and vulnerable.

In fact, I didn't even trust the evidence of my own senses.

I tried the door.

It was locked.

I glanced up and down that hallway. People approached. Not suited commission members, but wearing the jeans and shorts and skirts of the Portland public.

These were concerned citizens, expecting to attend a meeting. Even from a couple of dozen feet away, I could feel their petty personal issues and grievances like a miasma of light smog.

Hells, from three of them I could even feel that foul thing I find most counterproductive: idealism. Like rays of sunshine, breaking through the light smog.

Worse, what I didn't feel from any of them was rage. No one was there to *fight* for their cause. To make a scene, or even a point. They worst thing any of them wanted to do was speak sharply.

It was as though all I had been weaving and working towards had been undone. As though...

As though I'd spent weeks building a massive house of cards using no less than fifteen decks. And the morning I intended to knock it all down while recording the collapse on my phone, I came downstairs to find no house of cards at all.

Only fifteen decks. Still sealed.

I had to hope this analogy was only the exaggeration of severe disappointment. I had no way to gauge, though. Nothing like this had ever happened to me before.

I, whose tireless work and devotion to detail had produced the right circumstances for no less than six major workings in the two years previous.

Things like what was happening right then, they just did not happen to me.

Therefore, *this* did not *just happen.*

Someone had to be actively working against me. I had to find out who.

---

PARANOIA WASHED OVER ME IN A WAVE OF COLD SWEAT. I STOOD WITH my back to the cold, painted concrete wall of a minor hallway in Portland City Hall. Opposite the closed door of the room where no meeting would take place that day.

My mind raced as fast as my heart. My breaths came quick and shallow.

A dozen people approached. All seeming to be nothing more than good citizens of a democracy, about their civic duty. Attempting to attend a commission meeting, to ensure that their views are considered.

Half of them over sixty. Four of them women, two men. Dressed more formally, which for Portland meant that their short-sleeved shirts and blouses had buttons and collars. They wore jeans and long skirts, considering their shorts days behind them. They kept their hair neat.

All six had enough focus that they might be presenting false fronts. Any one of them might be part of my problem.

Three of the others were younger. Angrier. Not the kind of angry I needed, but with unfocused ire they intended to vent in lip service to ideals they didn't live.

Those three were nothing. Pawns, waiting for the hand of a player to move them about.

The three idealists were young. A trio of college age women. The sort who will become politicians or lobbyists or party bosses, once the shine of their idealism wears away.

I felt my hand twitch with the urge to raise that I might mark them. Idealists such as those three would make marvelous tools, under the right conditions.

Nothing swells discontent in others faster than unchecked idealism.

I stayed my hand because the paranoia whispered that they might be lures. They might bear hidden markers of my opponent.

After all, that someone worked against me did not mean a personal motivation. They might have been working against my project without knowing it was my hand moving the pieces.

If I were operating blind in such a situation, I would send in marked lures such as the three idealists.

I settled for noticing that one carried a notebook bearing the Portland University logo. If I wanted to find them again, I needed only seek the political clubs on that campus. Sooner or later, they'd turn up.

In the moment, though, I scanned them all with my eyes once more, checking for the most important detail of all.

Who noticed me?

I held still and waited. Watching. Trying to hear something beyond the desperate beating of my heart.

Every one of them turned toward the door, not toward me. They read the sign. Discussed their disappointment among themselves, if they came with a friend or three. Some even credited themselves for this postponement — the righteousness and passion of their arguments at past meetings — but even in the throes of paranoia, I could hear those claims ring false.

I didn't listen to their words though. I couldn't spare that much focus on the physical. I was too intent on the meaning behind their words. I was too involved in hearing their intentions, rather than their words.

And what I heard had nothing to do with me.

They all turned away from the meeting room and went about their business.

Not one of them spared me so much as a curious glance, let alone a gloating wink.

I remained invisible. Or rather, unnoticeable, which, honestly, is much better than actual invisibility.

The grip of paranoia eased.

I could not say for certain that the three college women were not lures, sent to catch me. But beyond that, I felt confident that none of those dozen citizens had worked against me in any meaningful way.

Which, honestly, was worse.

If one of that dozen had been my opponent, matters could have accelerated. We could have opposed one another directly. Held a battle of sorts right here in the building, with only one of us walking away.

Instead, the paranoia of the moment faded until I was left with the uncomfortable certainty that my opponent, or his agents, were somewhere about. Lying in wait for me.

*"Why 'his?'" Sebastian asked, and when I sighed, he chose to elaborate. "Why did you assume your opponent was male?"*

I assumed nothing of the sort. I used "his" in that instance because the English language lacks a properly genderless third person pronoun for referring to an individual instead of an object.

*"Wake up and smell the twenty-first century," Sebastian said, with more condescension than I cared for. "'They' and 'their' have been officially accepted by all reputable sources as serving that linguistic role."*

So, rather than confusing the issue in terms of the gender of my opponent, you would prefer I confuse the issue in terms of number of opponents?

*"I can't listen to this argument again," Eamon said.*

*"Just concede the point and move on,"* Harley implored. *"I'm more interested in the rest of what happened than I am in arguing gender politics."*

*"Gender has become a political issue,"* Sebastian said, *"because many politicians refuse to accept—"*

All right!

I was left with the uncomfortable certainty that my opponent, or one of *their* agents, were somewhere about. Lying in wait for me.

Better? May I continue then?

Very gracious of you.

I held my place there, against the wall, and waited for a time. Trying to ignore the foul stench of the abused oranges befouled for the cleaning solution that had recently been used on the floor.

But as is often the case, attempting to ignore something made me more aware of it. More so than would normally be the case, because the things I was waiting for were too few and far between to serve as distraction.

I was waiting for latecomers to the meeting. There were not many, and what few there were were too clearly innocent of all but a desire to learn what the commission was doing.

They lacked even issues of their own to present. They were the idly curious of the democratic process. Those trending toward middle age who found themselves with too much time and too few productive ways to spend it, so they had begun indulging odd curiosities.

Ah, any one of the ten or so stragglers might have become a useful tool to me. For though idle hands are said to fall more often to the uses of Eamon's patron, I and mine have uses for them as well.

I could not trust any of them enough to mark them. Any one of them, or all of them, might be tagged as lures by my unseen opponent.

I noted that no reporters arrived. Not even from a local college newspaper or radio station. Which meant that the commission had informed the press of the cancellation, if not the public.

And before any of you ask, yes I can tell a reporter from the public. The psychic difference between them is as noticeable as the difference between a southern drawl and an Irish lilt.

When ten minutes passed without a latecomer arriving, to turn away in disappointment, I was ready to at last make my move.

As I had mentioned, the door to the meeting room was locked. This was in keeping with the standard practice of all rooms of Portland City Hall, when they were not in use.

And with its meeting canceled, no one had any reason to bother with this room for the rest of the day.

Which meant that this room would be the perfect staging point for my investigation.

A LOCKED DOOR PRESENTS NO IMPEDIMENT TO THE LIKES OF US. AND yes, Sebastian, I include you in that statement. Were we not, the four of us, adepts of similar development along our diverse paths, we would not find nearly so much to talk about at these lunches.

So I trust the three of you will not consider it boastful to say that I unlocked the door, slipped inside, and locked it once more as soon as I felt certain no one was looking down the hallway.

Yes, I was confident in my unnoticeability. But this was not a moment to risk error.

With the door closed, the room was warm and dark. I smelled dust, and rotting bananas. A strange combination.

That sense from the hallway, as though I were in a mine under risk of collapse, continued here into the room with me. If anything, as my eyes adjusted, I felt even more confined.

The air conditioning was off in this room, and it was west-facing. Afternoon heat had seeped in.

I half-expected to hear the scuttle of rats. Instead I heard pipes, from a nearby washroom, as of a toilet being flushed. Beyond that, hardly even the sound of the building settling. Even the faint strains of traffic from outside were louder.

My eyes adjusted to the gloom, turning the darkness to more of a dim, late twilight.

The room was smaller than I expected. Rectangular, with the single door in the middle of one long side.

Three windows shaped like the room were set high in the opposite wall, with their blinds down. I could make out the wide meeting table perhaps twenty feet in front of me, at the end of a single aisle between two rows of chairs. Six chairs to a row.

Interesting. If the meeting had taken place, some of the concerned citizens would have had to stand.

I gnashed my teeth. The mere choice of rooms indicated how close I'd come to my goal. They commission clearly didn't want a strong public presence. Hells, if the press attended, the room would feel overcrowded.

Oh, so much wasted opportunity for greater tension.

Who dared to put a stop to it?

I didn't turn on the lights. There was always a chance, however slim, that the custodial staff might come in and deal with the rotting banana smell, which was clearly coming from an unemptied wastebasket off to my left.

I did not know the schedule of the custodial staff. I hadn't thought I'd need it. Though I noted to learn it for next time, just in case.

Now, though, I had work to do.

I attempted to center myself through a deep breath, but required three. The first two were lost to an urge to sneeze, brought on by the room's surprising amount of dust.

When was the last time this room was used?

In case that question mattered, I took a moment, still standing right where I was, and stretched forth my psychic tendrils to examine the room about me.

Rage, so red it bordered on purple. Venom. Indignation both righteous and selfish. Screaming matches. A thrown slice of tomato from someone's sandwich.

Chairs thrown back. Police officers moving to intervene...

Only six short weeks ago, this room was packed for a meeting of the Portland Housing Advisory Commission, in a heated battle between renters and landlords, with homeless advocates attacking all sides.

I came back to myself on my knees, half drunk from the afterglow of all that fury.

Oh, how did I not know of this meeting? How could such wondrously powerful passions fly about with no one in my sect the wiser?

I never even read about this meeting in the newspaper. Truly astounding. The effort someone must have gone to, to cover it up. Because surely someone in the editorial department of the *Oregonian* would've achieved orgasm at the thought of the headline *Housing Meeting Descends Into Food Fight*.

Well.

I had lost my opportunity to bring about a great work from what would have taken place here today — especially considering the groundwork that had been laid in this room beforehand — but I could certainly make use of the remnants of that housing meeting.

Moving slowly in the gloom, I made my way down the path between the audience chairs and around the meeting table, and finally to the large, executive roller chair in the center. This was the seat of the commission president. The focal point of not only the meeting itself, but much of the passion spewed from one direction or another.

With my left hand, I made the sign of Power Recognized at the chair, in acknowledgment of the role it served, and the role served by those who sat within it.

With my right hand, I made the sign of Power Claimed, and took the seat for myself, assuming the mantle implied by this position as well.

I eased down into the chair. Feeling the contours of faux leather adapting to my body. Listening to the soft expulsion of air from its cushions. I reached down and raised the seat, heightening my position, and allowing me to look down on all I surveyed.

I rested my elbows on the armrests, and steepled my fingers, looking about as though watching others take their place in my demesne.

Little actions, their significance as much psychological as psychic, but they were forming the first falling pebbles of the avalanche of power I intended to raise and loose.

With one psychic tendril, I formed an ectoplasmic gavel. I tapped that gavel three times on the table before me, hearing its ghostly rapping as much in my imagination as in my ears.

At that point, anyway.

"I now call this meeting to order," I said, fully claiming position of power.

With that, I extended my tendrils into the morass of echoing fury and began to siphon it inwards to myself.

Even as I did so, I almost sighed at the waste. Not the waste that had gone before during the housing meeting itself — though that was certainly bad enough — but the waste of those remnants of power.

Even the echoes of such fury are better spent on action than investigation. But I needed answers. And this power would get them for me.

I did not channel those lingering energies through myself. That might taint their purity. Rather instead, I brought them together before me in a globe of pulsing, purple energies.

So bright and beautiful their color and light extended dimly into the spectrum visible even to physical eyesight.

I drew them together slowly and carefully, to ensure that I missed not a jot of what they had to offer me.

Which, alas, was why I was only half-done when I heard keys jingle in the door handle.

## 11

## CLARK

It was strange, watching the gruesome foursome from the safety of behind the bar while Zed told his story. While Eamon and Sebastian had been talking, the other three interrupted at seemingly regular intervals. And when Zed started, they'd been giving him the same treatment.

And yet, as Zed's story moved along, either he anticipated their questions, or simply managed to do a better job of holding their attention. Because I would have sworn that a pin could have dropped in that bar and the only one who would have heard it was me.

Which was why I jumped when Sebastian suddenly raised his hand and called out, "Clark? Would you clear our empties?"

"What are you doing?" Zed growled, and I admit that the question sounded better coming from him than it would have from me.

"I'm tired of the clutter," Sebastian said, unabashed, as I approached with a tray. "Besides. I want another round, and I suspect I'm not alone in this."

"I've had enough beer for now," Eamon said, which got a frown from Sebastian, who mouthed something I didn't catch.

Eamon sighed. "But I suppose I could do with a Pepsi."

"Excellent," Sebastian said, louder over the clinking of glasses as I managed to fit them all on one tray, along with the empty, red plastic baskets from their food. He continued, "And I would like another Guinness, as, I suspect, would Harley."

"More fried tentacles and onion rings, too," Harley said with a nod.

"And I think some of your spicy fries," Sebastian said, giving me a wink that made my face warm.

All three looked at Zed.

Zed looked at me. "Pepsi."

"You got it, guys. Be just a minute."

I had to fight the urge to hustle away from that table, but loaded down as I was, I didn't dare. I heard them talking about something while I was dealing with the empties, but I missed what they were saying.

I had enough to do that I couldn't hear anything more from them until I was bringing their next round of food and drinks.

Of course, they were quiet then. They waited until I'd distributed everything before any of them spoke. And it was Sebastian who broke the silence, before I even left their table.

"How hard is it, Clark?" I almost thought that was innuendo, but he continued, "Having just the four of us here for lunch like this, once a week."

"I like you guys," I lied with a shrug, "and you do well by me. Could be much worse."

Sebastian nodded as though I'd said something more significant than the pablum of the small business owner reassuring regulars whose money was more welcome than they were.

In fact, I realized then that all four of them nodded. Sebastian was just the most overt. Eamon gave a small, quiet not. Harley's jaw jerked up and down, almost as though he were remembering something.

Zed, well, Zed's jaw went down, but it didn't come back up, the way a nod is supposed to. It was as though he changed his mind mid-nod. Or maybe, that half a nod was all my little response was worth.

Either way, we weren't continuing the conversation. So I tapped the table as a kind of acknowledgment, and made my way back behind the bar.

When I got there, I realized Zed was staring thoughtfully at me. Which, let me tell you, was more than enough to send the creeps up my back, down my front, and all around my sides.

It occurred to me then that, tapping my hand the way I had, might've been taken as a way of knocking with a gavel.

Maybe that was paranoia. Maybe not. I couldn't read anything in Zed's expression. I never could.

I couldn't move while he stared at me, though. I felt like a mouse, frozen by the hypnotic gaze of a snake. Not sure if I feared the strike, or would welcome its release from the tension singing through my body.

He turned away then, back to his companions. And when his attention shifted, it was like a physical pressure was lifted. I felt sweet relief flood me.

I swear. I almost wet my pants. I know I did break out in a cold sweat.

Broke my own rule about day drinking with a double shot of eighteen-year-old Macallan. Took me three tries to hold my hand steady enough to pour, without wasting good whisky all over the bar.

I savored the burn of the Macallan as it went down almost as much as I savored the smoke underlying the creamy taste.

They weren't paying any attention to me as I did those things. They kept their focus on their drinks and their food.

That was good. As long as I kept the tigers happy, they weren't likely to turn on me.

But I no longer had any illusions about these four. Not after today. They were something beyond. Something else. Something not quite human, like the rest of us.

But whatever magic they held, they paid a terrible price for it.

So I didn't envy them. I just wanted to avoid becoming their target. Me, and everyone I cared about.

Maybe I needed to do more, though, than serve them food and drinks.

These four, they represented real evil walking the streets of Portland. Hell, what Zed was talking about, that involved affecting the way the city was run, for no better reason than raising some kind of power to bring about his own kind of badness.

What's that old saying? Something about evil only needing good men to do nothing?

I wasn't so sure I was a good man. But maybe I needed to do more than nothing.

Maybe I needed to find these Carters. Talk to them.

But if I were going to do that, I needed to listen more. Needed to understand more.

I knew full well I'd be taking my life in my hands if I went looking for these Carters. Hell, I didn't even know if Carter was a title or a last name.

But whatever they were, I might have only one shot to find them and convince them to do something about the gruesome foursome. And that meant I needed to know as much as I could.

So I settled in behind the bar, pretended to work on my laptop — innocuous work stuff, in case one of the gruesome foursome found some way to check — and listened.

**12**

———

# ZED

I was caught between the physical and the metaphysical. Which might make a good conundrum for a mental exercise, but in terms of magical work, it was a bind.

Physically, I sat in the dust and warm gloom of a disused meeting room where the most remarkable characteristic was the cloying smell of a rotting banana in the nearby wastebasket.

Metaphysically, I sat amid the chaotic cluster of emotions lingering after that tumultuous housing advisory commission meeting. Gloriously purple in their passions.

Physically, I sat in the position of power. The commission president's executive roller chair in the middle of the table, raised as high as the pneumatics would go, where I could look down on both the chairs of other commission members, and those few seats available to the public in such a tight, confining room.

Metaphysically, I'd assumed that position of power for myself. My psychic tendrils were busy gathering the lingering power in my claimed demesne and knitting them together into a single, large ball of power that pulse so brightly purple even my physical eyes could see traces of it.

My attentions were split this way. My right hand held an ectoplasmic gavel that gained more solidity with each passing moment. My left hand clutched the armrest of my executive roller chair in just the way the president of the housing advisory commission had, during that meeting.

When I first heard the jingle of keys, I couldn't tell if I was hearing an echo of the past or an action in the present. And I was so busy I had trouble pulling enough focus to find out.

The door opened. In current time. Not during that past commission meeting, but as I sat there alone in the gloom.

My psychic tendrils snapped back into me with such force I jerked. I instinctively shifted all my attention to keeping hold of my gavel and my ball of gathered power.

The light switch clicked on.

I looked up.

A maintenance man stood in the doorway. Tall and pale, with a blond, Teutonic look and a jagged scar under his chin.

He stood straighter than most maintenance men I'd seen. As though his dark blue jumpsuit were a tailored Brooks Brothers ensemble. He carried a wastebasket lined with black plastic.

He didn't startle when he saw me. He just stepped all the way into the room and closed the door behind him.

He opened his mouth to speak.

I tapped my gavel, now physically present enough to ring out on the wooden table.

"Order. Order," I said. "We *will* follow Robert's Rules in this meeting, and the chair has not acknowledged you."

He tried to speak anyway, and looked surprised that he failed. Then realization spread across his face, and a matching realization likely spread across my own.

He had realized I had claimed the position of power here.

I realized that this was no maintenance man at all, but either my opponent, or an agent of my opponent.

"Point of order," he said, Bert, if his nametag was to be believed, apparently knew Robert's Rules well enough to know those words would let him speak. "The roll has not been called, nor your right to the gavel been established."

I should've been able to answer back immediately by pointing out that I'd just called the meeting to order, even if my phrasing hadn't been perfect.

But the problem was that he said those words with as much force as I'd put into mine.

He was trying to claim position of power.

And he'd managed to give me a solid psychic slap across the face as he did it.

I marshaled my forces quickly.

"You are late, and the meeting started without you. The chair is not responsible for informing you of what you've missed."

Inspiration hit me with a smile. I knew how I could force him to wait until I finished gathering the lingering power.

"Now be seated," I said, "while the chair finishes reviewing the minutes of the last meeting."

"Point of order," Bert said, without missing a beat. "The meeting cannot be called to order if a quorum is not present."

My ectoplasmic gavel dissolved and my position of power evaporated into nothing more than a chair at an empty table.

He'd used a clever trick. I'd been gathering the power left over from that commission meeting. Thus, when trying to apply Robert's Rules for my own power, I'd subjected myself to the rules of that commission.

And unfortunately, Bert was right. That commission could not gavel a meeting to order without a quorum present.

I still had the purple ball of gathered power, but I'd lost the ability to gain more anytime soon.

And Bert looked ready to challenge me for that ball of power.

"You did impressive work," he said, setting down his wastebasket. "The slow, smooth way you dug your claws into the planning and sustainability commission. I was nowhere near guessing your identity. I'd commend you for your cunning, if your goals weren't so foul."

"And what do you know about my goals?" I asked.

He gave a slight, one-shoulder shrug. "Maybe nothing."

"You're the one who got the meeting postponed, I presume."

He gave me an arrogant smile and a half-bow.

"Yes, well, Zed, if that is your real name, you aren't the only one with a modicum of influence around here."

"That's why you come as a janitor. You…" It hit me like a flash that left me smiling despite myself. "You were going to take all the juice out of the room through that banana peel, weren't you? Using the janitorial angle, rather than the commission angle. Not bad."

"Psychic trash, physical trash. Wouldn't have been as elegant as your approach, but it would've been faster. Less prone to interruption."

My own psychic tendrils might've felt a little stunned from their sudden snap back into my etheric body, but they recovered quickly enough to let me know I'd gathered about two-thirds of what could be gathered here without staying overnight.

"Tell you what, then," I said. "As a nod to a fellow player, I'll take what I've gathered and go. Leave you the rest. Seems only fair."

*"Seriously?" Eamon asked in disbelief. "You yield even an inch to an opponent and soon enough they've taken everything you once held dear."*

*"Not so sure I'd lay out the kind of extremes that Eamon does," Harley said, "but I agree in essence. Someone comes at you, you can't just hand over what they want. They'll come heavier next time."*

Sebastian? Care to throw in your two cents?

*"I'm more interested in finding out what you did next," Sebastian said, sipping at his beer and toying with his fries.*

All right. So the two of you with unasked for commentary have voiced your opinions. So let me ask you a question.

What on earth or in any hell you can imagine makes you believe I intended to leave without destroying my enemy?

I am allowed to present false offers, am I not?

Now, if I might continue.

Unfortunately, I could tell from the quirked smile on Bert's face that he didn't believe my offer any more than I did.

"Sure," he said. "I'm good with every part of that except the part where you leave with that purple ball of power there."

"So you're unwilling to be reasonable?" I said, giving him a flat look.

"I think it's time we stopped playing games and got down to business."

"Funny," I said, standing up. "I was just thinking the same thing."

---

*"Actually," Sebastian said, "I do have a question."*

Go ahead.

*"Well, things had obviously degraded to the point of combat. This Bert guy was even stupid enough to point it out. So. You were standing there with a mass of power already gathered. Power you said yourself would be better used aggressively than for investigation.*

*"So I guess I just don't understand why you bothered with a quip. Or why you bothered letting him finish his sentence. Why didn't you just hit him with one of those nasties you guys are always talking about?"*

*Eamon sighed. Harley shook his head.*

*"What?" Sebastian asked. "Honestly. Remember, guys. I'm a lover, not a fighter. So explain to me what I'm missing."*

Allow me.

There are two reasons. The first, and I would think the more obvious, was that the power I'd gathered was too valuable to waste in a single blast against a foe of unknown capabilities.

I wanted that power for later. I wanted that power to help me overcome the damage that had been done to my progress with the planning and sustainability commission.

The second reason was that, well, it's easier to channel one's thoughts and powers along combat lines when all of one's movements and actions operate in alignment with such activities.

Simple sympathetic magic. By moving and acting as a warrior — and in this capacity, the examples played out in movies and television influence the zeitgeist and carry more power than the movements and behaviors of actual warriors such as Navy SEALs — it becomes easier to wield the powers of war.

So yes, as Bert and I faced off in that dusty meeting room, we postured verbally for a moment as though we were on television. Because it was the quickest, easiest way to ensure our powers were flowing along the right lines.

"I'll give you one last chance," Bert said. "Release the ball of power and I'll let you walk away."

I shook my head. Wrapped two of my psychic tendrils around that ball of power and moved it behind me.

"Only one of us is walking away from this anyway. You know that."

"All right then," he said. "I had to try."

I almost lost time wondering about that statement. In the moment, I couldn't afford to worry about it. To assume that it was anything more than the posturing required for him to position himself as the "good guy" in the fight.

I had no problem with that. Fictional villains tend to win every fight but the most important one, and this fight wasn't anything more than of middle-of-the-story impact.

Figured that gave me an edge.

Looking back, though, I have to admit. Bert seemed sincere. I mean, he hadn't exactly been hiding behind a poker face through our little dialog. And he honestly sounded disappointed that I was going to make him fight for what little I planned to scrape together out of the ashes of my plans.

Well, whether he was sincere or not, his assuming the "good guy" role gave me the moment I needed to strike first.

I hit him with Responsibility.

He was dressed as a janitor. He had aligned himself with the role of custodial agent before even entering this room, and he'd prepared himself psychicly to use that role for magic. So I figured it was where he was most vulnerable.

Responsibility can be a crushing weight. And here he was, the sole custodian in a room teeming with dust and neglect. The rank stench of that rotting banana like a tsunami of accusation — *Get! To! Work!*

He dropped his key ring. Swayed in place. Sweat broke out on his forehead, as he shook with the struggle against the overpowering need to forget about me and start cleaning.

I started around the table and toward the door. Figured I'd grab his keys along the way. Never knew when they might come in handy.

He was mumbling something. Probably a counterspell. More the fool, Bert, then. If he took concentration away from fighting my spell, he'd start cleaning before he'd do anything else.

"Seven…" he said louder, which was strange enough that I stopped in the aisle between the audience chairs, maybe two steps from him. "Seven … GEE!"

He shook himself and started panting like a track star, but he was smiling. And I didn't like that at all.

"Code … seven … gee…" He rolled his neck. "Reporting a crime in progress or evidence of a past crime takes precedence over all other activities."

He pulled out a freaking walkie-talkie.

"And gee, here I've found someone guilty of trespassing and unlawful entry."

"You have no evidence of that," I said, quickly, trying to think of a way out of this that wouldn't end with me in jail.

"I had to unlock the room to get in," he said, smiling even wider. He raised the walkie-talkie.

I crossed the distance between us and knocked the walkie-talkie from his hand. But I'd committed the classic blunder. The one common to audiences watching stage magicians from time immemorial.

I'd paid so much attention to the hand he wanted me to look at that I'd lost track of what his other hand was doing.

I knocked the walkie-talkie away.

He hit me with a taser.

I'd done too much sweating, once I'd found the meeting postponed. My skin, my clothes, so much dried salt that I was probably twice as vulnerable as normal.

*"That's not quite how it works," Eamon said, but I waved him to silence.*

May I not have any artistic license at all then?

*"You wouldn't allow me any," Sebastian pointed out, and even I had to concede the point.*

Well, whether my own sweat had worked against me or not, that taser blast jolted through me harder than anything else I could remember.

I'd even once committed the error common to curious children, involving a fork and a power outlet.

The taser was worse.

Every muscle in my body locked up so tight it was a wonder I didn't crack any teeth. The pain was an evil, living thing, seeming to bite me everywhere at once, but adding an overlay of more in a rapid succession of chomps from my face to my toes.

I think I made some kind of grunting sound. The only expression of pain I could make, while I had no control of any of my muscles.

But I did have my mind. After the initial momentary shock, I kicked myself out of my body.

Bert's eyes tracked me as I did. His lips quirked in a small frown.

"Damn," he said, "you are adept, aren't you?"

I was trying to gather enough together to hit him. And I was ready to dip into that ball of power to do it.

"All right," he said. "This is it. No more."

He pulled a nine-millimeter pistol out of his sock. Which means he'd pulled off an impressive feat just getting that into the building.

"Release the ball and I'll take it and walk away. If not" — he held up the pistol — "I'll plant this on you and give you to the cops. I'll get the power anyway, and you'll get a criminal record."

I wasn't sure he was adept enough to hear me speak from the astral, so I just gave him the most skeptical expression I could.

"I swear," he said, forming a kind of pyramid with the fingers of both hands, "upon the magic that serves me, and upon the powers I serve. Cede that ball of power to me, and I will leave you in peace for this day, taking no more actions against you and yours before the sun next rises."

I hated myself for doing it, but I nodded.

I released those tendrils that still clung to the ball of power. He issued tendrils of his own to claim it. He recovered his keys, his walkie-talkie, and his bucket.

He left without even taking away that damned rotting banana.

I had to smell that awful odor as my body finally shook off the worst of the effects of the taser.

I ached all over. I had lost both my meeting and what little I'd hoped to salvage.

In fact, I managed only one small victory before Bert left me to my sorrows.

I slipped a tracking element into the ball of power before he claimed it. A tracking element that would slither up one of his tendrils and into his etheric body.

After all. I'd made no promises of peace.

13
—————

## CLARK

Something about the way Zed said those last six words. *I'd made no promises of peace.* I found it jarring enough that I jostled my laptop.

He sounded, well, he sounded just the way I imagined serial killers sounded when they said they were ready to go on the hunt.

And he never did say what his sect used all that power to *do*...

Eamon and Sebastian both glanced at me when I jostled the laptop, so I slapped my hand on the bar and muttered loud imprecations about the bad Wi-Fi.

I didn't see their reactions. Couldn't afford to look at them head-on. But from the corner of my eye I did see them turn their attention back to their conversation.

It was a bad choice of things to blame, to be honest. My Wi-Fi at the bar has always been good. I'm too much of a geek — and I cater to too many geeks — to allow for bad Wi-Fi.

But hey, even a good connection had bad moments, right?

Just to be safe, I shook my head, grimaced, muttered "Come on," and fetched myself a glass of water. As though my attention was on anything but the conversation of the gruesome foursome.

"You tracked him down, I presume," Eamon said. "How long did it take you?"

"Didn't," Zed said. "Couldn't. By the time I'd made it safely out of the building, Bert — if that was his name — had found the tracking element and defeated it."

Zed polished off the last of one of his Pabst Blue Ribbons before taking a sip from his Pepsi.

"Sounded like a Carter," Harley said. "The 'good guy' posturing. Claiming the high road, even though they don't really follow it."

"Plus," Sebastian said, "he used more trickery than magic. I've always thought that Carters got queasy around magic."

"That could just have been opportunism," Eamon said. "The taser in that case led to the path of least resistance."

"He was lying about some of it," Zed said. Shook his head. "Had to be. Overstating his case, I mean."

"How so?" Sebastian asked.

"If he and his knew as much as he pretended, were as involved as he pretended, then why did his wait six weeks to claim the remnants from that housing commission meeting?"

"Good point," Harley said. "The smart move would be to snatch it at the first opportunity."

"Ergo," Eamon said, "Friday was his first opportunity. But he did arrive ready to act."

"Could have been a scheduling issue," Sebastian said with a half-shrug.

"You mean the alignment of the stars and moon?" Harley asked.

"I was thinking about when he could juggle the custodial schedule in such a way to allow him access."

"I don't think he discovered the power in that room until the meeting was postponed," Zed said. "Or at least until the meeting was announced as taking place in that room."

"The logic holds," Eamon said, "and would explain why he hadn't claimed the power before."

"So," Harley said. "I'm Bert. I track the influences on local Portland government, and discover a committee ready to come to blows over issues, on the very day they're supposed to meet."

"I go check out the room in advance," Eamon said, picking up the thread, "maybe to do the kind of psychic tuning you spoke of, Zed."

"I discover," Zed continued, "that this room is already teeming with power congruent with the goals of whoever was manipulating the commission. That is, the actual me."

"But," Sebastian said, which apparently surprised Eamon, "I'm not in a position to do anything about that lingering power right away. Not if I'm going to postpone the meeting first."

"Just so," Eamon said, approvingly, and getting an eyeroll from Sebastian as he continued. "Postponing the meeting takes precedence. Then it's just a question of aligning myself for the janitorial role, and waiting until the room is empty to come in and sweep up the remnant power."

"Sounds like Carter behavior to me," Harley said.

"Could be," Eamon said, sounding less convinced. "But that pyramid shape Bert formed with his hands..."

"I was just wondering that myself," Sebastian said.

"And I agree," Zed said. "Whatever fragment of the Illuminati has gathered in this area and moved against you two" — he pointed at Eamon and Sebastian — "appears to be moving against me and mine, as well."

"Allied in this, then?" Sebastian asked?

"Allied," Zed said, clinking glasses with Sebastian and Eamon before sharing a drink.

"That doesn't address the issue of whether or not they're Carters," Eamon said, lowering his Pepsi. "Though I doubt it. The ones I dealt with were clearly manufacturing and dealing crystal methamphetamine. Hardly the sort of behavior we've come to expect from Carters."

"They do err on the side of the goody-good," Sebastian said. "Which means it would be inconsistent with their general *modus operandi* to arm a man with arrows and set him up to murder one of the most beautiful creatures ever to grace this planet."

"*Modus operandi*?" Eamon said, with as much of a smile as I'd ever seen on his face before.

"What?" Sebastian asked, fluttering his eyelashes. "Am I so pretty I'm not allowed to have a brain?"

"Well," Eamon replied, "you were the one addressing inconsistencies in patterns of behavior…"

Harley smacked the table with a big hand. "Can we get back on topic?"

"I'd prefer it," Zed said. "I did take the opportunity to speak to others of my sect. Not to address my own failures of the week, but to see if any others had seen signs of a new sect of players in the Portland area who might be inclined to move against us."

"And?" Sebastian asked.

"Nothing," Zed said, with a single shake of his head. "What's more, their projects were all seeing signs of smooth sailing."

"So," Eamon said, "indications then are that this fragment of the Illuminati might not be moving against our covens and sects, but against the four of us."

"That doesn't make sense, though," Sebastian said. "While we are, the four of us, fairly impressive adepts, we're none of us leaders."

Eamon cleared his throat.

"Are you the head of your coven?" Sebastian asked, clearly already knowing the answer.

Hell — which I was starting to think I wanted to stop saying — even I knew the answer to that one. They'd talked earlier about a woman being in charge of Eamon's coven. A woman Sebastian wanted to bang, but honestly, that didn't say anything about her.

"You know I am not," Eamon said shortly. "But that does not mean I will accept being depicted as someone who is not a leader. I am, have led, and will again lead."

"I was talking about holding the role of leader," Sebastian said with a sigh. "Not having the qualities of a leader."

"Whatever," Harley said. "Sebastian's right. We're high up in our respective groups, but we aren't the leaders. So why pick us to move against?"

I thought of something they all had in common, but I sincerely hoped that none of them thought of it.

Goodness knew that I had nothing to do with any moves against them, magical or otherwise. Hell, I mean heck, I didn't even know magic was real until that day.

What made it worse, of course, was that I was now thinking of taking action against them. If I could find a safe way to do it.

"Harley," Zed said. "We need to hear about last night. We need to know what happened. It may be more important than you think."

Harley laughed. A big, booming sound that lacked even a trace of humor.

"More important than I think?" He shook his head. "Not sure it could *get* more important than I think."

And Harley started to tell his story.

**14**

---

# HARLEY

YOU GUYS CAN CALL YOURSELVES "SECTS" AND "COVENS" ALL YOU LIKE. My group, we know what we are and we're not afraid to admit it.

We're a cult.

And as a cult, our goals are pretty simple. We *will* be responsible for bringing the Old Ones across the veil to take their rightful places once more.

R'lyeh *will* rise.

Mad Azathoth *will* play his pipes.

And dread Cthulhu *will* walk the earth.

*"All right, all right,"* Sebastian said, *waving his hands as though to stop a fight. "You guys came down on me hard for proselytizing, and you were going to let him go on like this?"*

*"He has a point,"* Zed said. *"We all know who you are and what you stand for."*

Very well. But consider that these are our ultimate goals, when you hear me talk about last night, what happened, and why it matters.

The day started well. I rose close to noon and dined first on three eggs that cracked bloody into my mixing bowl.

A small thing, but an indication that we had been reading the signs properly, and that the stars were coming into alignment in the way we predicted.

*"But there were no special conjunctions last night,"* Eamon said. *"My group watches the stars as well, and last night was nothing special."*

Nothing special here. However, Yog Sothoth knows the gate. Yog Sothoth is the gate. Yog Sothoth is key and guardian of the gate.

*"Seriously, Harley,"* Sebastian said. *"Proselytizing!"*

As you would have it. But it is through the starry wisdom of Yog Sothoth, as revealed in the book that shall not be named here, that we found an alignment that crosses the boundaries of this world and another.

Without risking more complaints from Sebastian, suffice to say that there are stars in Andromeda that aligned just so with stars in our own galaxy and stars in ... certain other places that provided us an opportunity no one expected to occur in our lifetimes.

If we succeeded, we would *undo the sinking of R'lyeh.*

Not merely raise it up once more from the depths of the seas, as others have tried before us, but we would have conformed this very reality to a world in which the great lost city of R'lyeh was never sunk in the first place.

It is not proselytizing to reveal that Cthulhu would never have been trapped, dead and dreaming, in a city that never sank beneath the waves.

Father Dagon. Mother Hydra. The roles of the deep ones.

This world would have been a very different place today, had we succeeded.

And when my day started yesterday, I had every reason to believe we would succeed.

It started with those three bloody eggs in my mixing bowl confirming for me that we'd read the signs correctly. I even paused my cooking to call the chief of my cult and inform him.

His eggs had come up bloody as well.

*"Gross, by the way"* Sebastian muttered, *but I don't think he meant an interruption.*

Perhaps. But important nonetheless.

As my day continued, I had many small things to do in preparation for the rites we would perform that night. And throughout my day, everything seemed to be going just right.

I split six stumps of old hickory for the bonfire we'd need, and all six stumps split dry as though we'd seasoned them for six years.

Our cult herbalist contacted me. He'd run short of saltpeter, asafetida, and sulfur, and needed me to make stops along the way to pick up supplies. But the amounts he needed were those I already possessed in my own cabinet.

I began to feel as though I could do no wrong. I felt an impulse to grab extra pillar candles, purple and black, just in case more were needed.

When I swung by that small occult store on southeast 108$^{th}$ for those candles, I hit every green light along the way, and all three police vehicles I saw were traveling different directions than I was.

In fact, things were going so well, that I completed all my small tasks early.

I found myself with two hours to kill, before the sun would begin to set and it would be time to head out into the rural part of Tualatin and our ritual site.

It was a warm, clear day for spring, and I felt a good kind of tension flowing through my muscles. The kind that me want to build something or destroy something.

If I'd had enough time, I might've run home and built that brick barbecue I've been thinking about since that last snowfall.

But I didn't have that much time.

Plenty of time to destroy something. Or someone. And destruction would be in alignment with the energies I'd need later that night.

But I couldn't let myself do that either. Not yesterday. Not when so much was riding on the rites we would perform that night.

No. I couldn't risk something going wrong on a side mission of chaos and destruction, making me miss the big event. I may not lead our cult, but I am the right claw. I am too important to risk that way.

So I tried to shunt my energies into planning. And I knew just where to do it. A small café in a place of loss and decay.

I drove my ancient but mighty — and fully loaded — pickup truck down to that mall on the edge of Tualatin. Only six miles or so from the ritual site, when the time came.

This mall is not the big one, with the huge movie theater. No, this is the small one. Only a half-mile further from the freeway, but that might as well have been the distance to Kathmandu, when it came to shopping.

The small mall always reeked broken dreams. It was a two-story type, with four spokes built around a round, central hub.

All four anchor stores were the kind of department stores who had commanded both respect and admiration back in the '80s. Now, two of them were closed and the other two were on life support.

I parked on the outer edge of the parking lot, with rows and rows of empty space between myself and other vehicles. This was more about an old hunting habit than about saving my rough old beast of a truck from further dings and scratches.

By parking far away, I got to truly survey the place I approached.

This was a Tuesday afternoon. The cars were arrayed in two groups. One group, closer to the entrance. Mostly older vehicles, showing signs of wear. Many of them likely on their second or third owners. And paint jobs. Even from where I parked I could almost smell hints of rust coming from them.

The other group was off to my left, closer to the border of the street, and conspicuously close to a Tri-Met station with insufficient parking.

Newer cars there. Better tended cars, too. Cars whose drivers probably never set foot inside this mall, for fear that someone would see them.

Another bad sign for the mall. It wasn't defending its borders from other predators.

I was dressed to blend in. Cargo shorts, plaid shirt with the sleeves rolled up to the elbow. Sneakers, instead of work boots. My notebook in one hand.

I was almost to the entrance of the mall when my phone rang, carrying with it the first sign of anything going wrong that day.

"Yes?" I said as I answered.

"Where are you?" The voice was that of my cult leader himself, and he sounded troubled.

"Nearby, but not too near."

"The meat's gone bad. It'll ruin dinner."

The sacrifice had escaped? But that wasn't, or shouldn't have been, possible.

"I don't understand," I said, shocked. "It looked good last night "

No, I hadn't been the one responsible for holding the sacrifice in preparation for the ritual, but I had contacted ... those responsible just the night before. And I'd been assured that everything was well in hand.

"That was last night," he said, practically spitting with anger. "Today *no meat* would be better than what we have."

I blew out a sharp breath. I knew what was coming, and I wasn't going to wait to be asked.

"Want me to pick up a chicken on the way home?"

"Only if you want to eat tonight."

Damn. So I was the *only one* in a position to get us a sacrifice? What the hell was going on with everyone else today?

"I'll take care of it," I said.

"I know you will." He hung up.

I turned and trotted back to my truck. I concealed my notebook, then dug a spare tarp out from under the split hickory logs and put in on the floor of the passenger side of my truck. From under my seat, I pulled out my personal emergency kit and filled a syringe with enough tranquilizer to take down a linebacker.

I reparked closer to the mall entrance.

And then I went to look for a sacrifice.

---

WHETHER IT'S DEEP IN THE BACKWOODS OF OREGON, OR IN A MALL IN

Tualatin, hunting is pretty much the same. Approach-wise, I mean. Different tools, of course, but you need to take the same approach.

Now, Sebastian talked about this earlier, a might. He said it all came down to patience and timing. And he's not all wrong there.

*"Gee, thanks," Sebastian said, rolling his eyes the way he liked to do when he thought we weren't taking him seriously.*

But maybe hunting and seduction don't have as much in common as he thinks. Because when it comes to hunting, first, you need to blend in.

Stand out as wrong or different, or even worse come off like a predator, and all the prey goes running soon as they catch a whiff.

*"Well," Sebastian said, "that does have parallels in—"*

*"Please, Sebastian," Zed said, not taking his eyes off me. Zed seemed extra intense once I started talking about a sacrifice. "We can debate hunting and seduction next time. Right now, Harley's tale may be critical to all our goals. And perhaps even our safety."*

*"I was thinking the same thing," Eamon said, looking even more serious than normal himself. Which was saying something.*

Now, I already had one advantage on the blending-in score. I was already dressed in suburban camo. The cargo shorts and plaid shirt with the sleeves rolled up. Wearing my beard thick and heavy the way I do, in that combination of shirt and shorts I'd be about as hard to spot as Zed. At least, in most Pacific Northwest crowds.

And I needed every edge I could get. Hunting for a sacrifice, properly done, was a job I should have had days to complete. A week, if possible. But I only had hours, and only a few of those.

So patience wasn't on my side. And timing would be something I'd have to manufacture, not wait for.

To be honest, I should've realized right then and there that our loss of a sacrifice was a sign of enemy action. Something that big going wrong? After the way all the signs had been pointing my way?

No way we lost a sacrifice to "bad luck."

Not as though we're a bunch of amateurs. We don't need sacrifices all that often, but when we do we're pretty good at handling our shit.

At the time, though, I couldn't afford to worry about the whys and wherefores. I had to get the job done.

Part of blending in was the look. I had that. The rest of blending in was a character. I decided to play it as though I were a guy early to a date, expecting to meet his girl in the food court.

So I smiled as I pushed through the glass doors, into refrigerated air that smelled like watch cleaner and something old and wet. My shoulders set back and my stride confident. Felt like my smile was as bright as the mall lighting. If anyone met my eye, I smiled wider and nodded a greeting. If they threw me a hello of some kind, I'd send it right back at 'em.

*"Now* that *is a disturbing mental image," Sebastian said, but I didn't waste time answering him.*

Mall was busy where I came in. One of the two remaining anchor stores was having a big spring sale. Small clusters of families bustled in and out, usually ordered about by a strong mother figure. Or, in some cases, vaguely wrangled by a pleading, desperate mother figure.

*"What kind of sacrifice were you looking for?" Eamon asked. "Male or female? Any age or virginity requirements?"*

We only take adults. Kids don't have enough umph. That virginity thing would be good, but probably not the way you mean it.

The way we look at it, a sacrifice with no scars is the best kind. One that hasn't been wounded or injured. Or even been cut open surgically, if we can find it, though that's less important. Common surgeries doesn't usually involve a lot of emotional investment.

To us, at least, spilling virgin blood means that we're the first people to spill that person's blood in any meaningful way.

That's one of the reasons we avoid the goth crowd. Incidence rates of cutting and sexual bloodletting are too high in that demographic. Too high a chance that we'd find someone already used up.

Metalheads and gangbangers aren't much better. They get into too many fights. Waste their blood in senseless, but *committed* violence.

No. What I was looking for was someone between the ages of, say, eighteen and … maybe twenty-five. If a woman, she hasn't given birth.

Shy types are best. The risk-avoidant. The world makes them hesitate, so they don't get hurt. Which means they don't tend to waste their blood before we can spend it properly.

I wasn't really looking for my target yet, though. I just wandered through the menswear, pretending to consider fragrances for my date and looking idly at shirts and slacks. I made a point of asking a young saleslady about the current fashion trends, as though I were nervous about what I was wearing for my date.

I didn't let her sell me a new shirt, but I did let her sell me a cologne. Didn't need it. Wouldn't use it. But it gave me a bag to carry around, with a receipt I could show, if I had to.

More camouflage.

When I left the store, I started actually looking around for prey. The crowds were sparse now, mostly groups of twos and threes, either busily about their business or more involved in socializing than shopping.

Apparently this was still the hangout of one of the local high schools. By the time I made it down to the food court — passing more empty storefronts than running stores — I'd seen maybe sixty people, and two-thirds of them were likely underage.

This was no good. I didn't want someone that young.

The food court itself wasn't bad, for a mall. They had a decent assortment of eateries, including a ribs place that served food I'd be willing to eat. In a pinch. If it weren't for the fact that the whole area smelled like french fries and hot dog water.

The food court took up the whole hub. An octagonal shape, under a big, spiderweb dome of paneled glass. Polarized, to keep the food court from turning into an oven in the summertime.

Kind of pretty, though. Lots of light.

Lots of auditory reflections, too. Maybe forty people total were eating or hanging out, scattered across an array of orange, plastic tables, but the clatter of their trays and the clashing of their conversations were louder than they should've been.

I stopped at the edge of the food court. Made a slight show of looking about, then checking my watch, then looking about again.

I stared at the nothingness between a group of chattering high school girls — cheerleader types with bright smiles and bright clothing — and a fortysomething loser who was trying not to get caught watching those girls.

I kept up the show of what I'd been pretending to do — thinking for a moment, even biting my lip as I did — before taking out my phone and pretending to set an alarm, then looking around hopefully one more time.

In my mind, though, I focused on that fortysomething guy.

He was pale and sweaty. Balding. Sagging. His jeans were too big through the legs and too tight through the waist. His tee shirt had something to do with dragons, but it was faded and he'd been thinner when he bought it.

He'd been eating nachos, and still had cheese on his fingers and his lips.

But his eyes. His eyes were the key. His eyes would tell me if he was a predator himself — perhaps the disgusting type who had plans for one or more of those giggling, bouncing teenage girls — or the type who was every bit as much in disguise as I was. The type who wanted to do some bloodletting of his own.

His eyes would also tell me if he was nothing more than the loser he appeared to be.

Under other circumstances I wouldn't care one way or the other. But today, oh, I needed this guy to be a loser. Because he seemed just the type who lived only the dreams of others, from the safety of his couch.

The blood of such a one would be *pristine*.

I approached the girls. Took note that they'd finished their fast food snacks, and were lingering over conversation and sodas.

They didn't even notice me until I was maybe five steps from their table. And even then, they didn't look up until I stopped at their table.

Oh, they were innocent, though. Two of them still smiling, eyes wide open with the certainty that the world was a sweet place that adored them and would see them home safely every night. One narrowed her eyes as though considering me the kind of threat her mother or teachers warned her about.

The last one actually looked me over as though appreciating the view. I didn't address her when I spoke.

"'scuse me," I said with a smile. "Have you four been here for a few minutes?"

"Yeah," one of the bright shiny ones said. "There was nothing on the table when we got here though."

"Oh," I said, trying to sound chagrined, "nothing like that. I was wondering. Have any of you seen a blonde woman? About so tall. Thirtyish. Very attractive. Probably wearing a pale green sundress."

They all shook their heads, in a cascade of flying hair.

"Friend of yours?" asked the one who was trying to be flirty.

"Yes," I said. "That's all right, though. I'm early. Just wanted to make sure she wasn't even earlier, or we might chase each other around the mall all afternoon."

The shiniest one tried to say something, but the flirty one wiggled her hand in a let-me gesture.

"What's her name?" the flirty girl asked.

"Tricia."

"Well," she said, eyeing me, "if we see Tricia, you want us to give her a message?"

"I should be back before she's due to arrive," I said. "Please though. If she beats me here, would you tell her that Hank is over at the bookstore and will be along in a moment?"

"I'd be happy to. Hank."

The other three girls started giggling.

"Thanks," I said, as though I didn't know why they were giggling. "I owe you one."

As I turned away, the flirty one muttered, "Wouldn't mind collecting *that* debt."

The girls didn't matter, though. I turned away in the right direction to let me see the fortysomething guy.

He was watching the girls out of the corner of his eye, with his focus on the shiniest one.

And the look in his eyes was sexual yearning.

He was perfect.

---

NOW, LOSING A SACRIFICE WE'D HAD ALL BOUND AND READY, THAT WAS bad on a scale you really want to avoid.

But for me to turn around and find what looked like another perfect sacrifice in less than an hour's searching? Even in prime hunting territory like that old mall, it just felt like another good sign on a day that had been full of good signs for me.

I felt as though Yog Sothoth himself was aligning the spheres for our sacrifice.

That's facetious, of course Yog Sothoth would do no such thing. Positive signs are the results of our own good preparatory magic, not acts of divine intervention.

Even a fool knows that the gods are indifferent at best and hostile at worst. While they remain where they are, that is. Where they were consigned by the Elder—

*Sebastian faked a cough around the word "proselytizing," then pretended to clear his throat.*

All right. The point is, finding that fortysomething guy in the food court felt like another good sign.

But there was also a solid chance that he wasn't just my *best* option. He might be my *only* worthwhile option. So I—

*"Theory question," Eamon said, and when I nodded, he continued. "One of those cheerleaders might have been eighteen. So why were they not an option?"*

*"Prying one loose from a pack is never easy," Zed said.*

*"Sure it is," Sebastian said. "Depending on who's doing the prying."*

*"I'm more curious about Harley's answer," Eamon said.*

Simple. Cheerleaders are athletes. Athletes push themselves. Get scrapes. Break limbs. So even if all four of those four girls were emotionally stable and not prone to fights or bad decisions, any one of those girls might be hiding scars under her clothes. From wounds suffered because of her emotional commitment to her athletics.

Wasted blood.

That fortysomething guy, though. He didn't look like a man who'd ever broken a sweat because of physical effort.

So, as I was saying, I didn't want to spook him. But I knew he wasn't leaving his table while those girls were at theirs, and I was pretty sure I'd just ensured that the girls would stay there until I got back.

So I wandered into the bookstore. Pathetic thing, really. Awful, New Age guitar music piped in over the speakers. More gadgets and gizmos and tchotchkes than books. Smelled like decent coffee from its coffee shop, which explained why more people were over in that part of the store than in the book-shopping sections.

I grabbed some bit of fluff with a dragon on the cover. Or in the title. Or both, maybe. I just grabbed the first thing I saw that involved a dragon, in case I needed a little extra bait for the fortysomething guy.

Wandered around for a few more minutes, idly pretending to shop, before paying. Cash, of course. I only ever paid cash while hunting. And I made sure I got a separate bookstore bag. Carrying two bags looked better to security guards than carrying only one.

In my experience, security guards trust shoppers more than they trust people who hang out at malls.

As I made my way back to the moderately busy, surprisingly noisy food court, I kept looking around. As though trying to spot Tricia. Let my expression get a little more worried now.

The fortysomething guy was still at his table. Getting a little bolder with his glances now, even though three-fourths of his eye candy was gone.

Well. Gone from their table, anyway. Given what happened next, I have little doubt that they were nearby, watching.

The flirty girl was still there, sitting on her table with her feet on her chair. Sipping through her straw and trying to get me to notice her.

I was just entering the food court when I pretended to get a text message. Made a show of juggling my bags while I checked my phone.

I sighed. Sagged a bit. Pretended to send a text message while shaking my head and looking sad.

"Bad news?" the flirty girl asked, approaching me while the fortysomething guy watched her walk with the intensity of a football fan watching the big game.

"She's not coming," I said with a sigh. "She got held up at work. Again."

"Her loss," she said, but I was still staring at my phone screen as though rereading a bad message.

"This was going to be our third date," I said. "Tricia always seems so interested, but her work…"

"Hey," the flirty girl said, snapping her fingers to get me to look up. "I mean it. Her loss. She's not here." She smiled. "And maybe my gain. 'Cause I am."

I looked her up and down as though actually considering a skinny, too-young thing like her. If she really wanted to chase older men, she'd have to learn to stop overdoing her makeup. Hair was all right, though. Wild and electric blue. Went with the pierced nostril to create a 'wild girl' image for her. Some guys would go for that.

"What's your name?"

"Taylor."

"And just how old are you, Taylor?" I asked, trying to sound skeptical, but maybe curious.

"Eighteen," she lied easily. My guess was three months shy of seventeen. She had Leo written all over her, and something in her manner told me she wasn't even within a year of eighteen yet.

"You're still too young for me."

"Bet I can prove you wrong."

Oh, hells. This girl was all bark and no bite. I could feel it. She was acting. Putting on a show for her friends. She probably wasn't even a cheerleader, like the others. She was the friend who watched from the crowd and cheered them on.

Naïve innocence rolled off her in waves stronger than her flowery perfume.

Damn it. If she were older, she might actually make a good sacrifice. And times were desperate.

This was a girl testing her boundaries. Maybe I could...

No.

She was too young. She needed to mature more before she'd be a worthy sacrifice. And given what was at stake that night, I couldn't risk bringing an unworthy sacrifice. Even one that came willingly to my hand.

But I didn't mean I couldn't make use of her.

I moved my head so that her blue hair blocked my mouth from the fortysomething guy's eyeline.

"You're cute," I said to Taylor. "But you're too young for me. Tell you what, though. If you're still interested in, say, five years, look me up. Name's Hank Habersham. There's only one of me on Facebook with a beard like mine, so I'm easy to find."

Taylor actually bounced at the suggestion of postponing her big adventure. Smiled even wider. Pretty sure I saw relief in her eyes.

"I will! I'll friend you, so you can see what you're missing. And maybe I can change your mind early."

"Well, you can always try," I said, smiling right back.

Then I did the important things.

I pointed down the spoke off the hub that would lead to my car. Hand high, so the fortysomething guy could see the gesture. My head, though, was still hidden from him by Taylor's.

"I think your friends went that way," I said. Then held up five fingers, again in full view of our observer. "Remember. Five years."

"I'll remember. Hank Habersham." And she strutted as she walked away. With as much wiggle in her hips as she could manage.

As she did that, I locked eyes with the fortysomething guy.

Before he could look away, I nodded a greeting.

His eyes widened. Spooked. Damn it. Must've thought ... well, it didn't matter what he thought.

He tried to get up, but he was too big and awkward to move that easily. I closed the distance between us before he even left his table.

"Hey," I said, trying to make it sound like a calm greeting. Even gave him a smile.

"I didn't do nothin'," he said, voice trembling as though he expected a beating.

Had he endured many beatings? I hoped not. If there was passion in those beatings...

I didn't have time to worry about it.

"Hey," I said, then said it a couple of more times, trying to put him at ease. "I'm not here to give you a hard time. I'm here 'cause I need your help."

"You. Need *my* help."

"I do," I said, then leaned in and lowered my voice like we were co-conspirators. "You saw those girls? The hot young things?"

"Yeah," he said, still sounding like he knew he'd been caught doing something he shouldn't.

"Those girls, they're going to meet me at my car in five minutes. Come back to my place for a little party, if you know what I mean."

"Good for you," he said, his tone not giving an inch.

"Could be good for *us*," I said, smiling. "There are *four* of them, man. I needed to promise I'd bring a friend. But my boy's stuck at work, so I'm a friend short right now."

"And you want..." He shook his head. And when this guy shook his head, the ripples went across his jowls and most of his torso. "Naw. No way. They want a guy with muscles like you. Not a ... not a guy like me."

"Hey, you're missing the beauty of the whole thing," I said. "These are young, adventurous girls. What they want is a *man*." I nodded at different groups of high schoolers visible from where we stood. "They've warmed up with *boys*. Now they're ready for the real thing. They're ready for guys like us."

He wanted to believe me. His desperation was almost as strong as his body odor. But he wasn't ready.

"Hey," he said. "What about that Tricia you're supposed to have a date with?"

Good. I knew he'd been listening in earlier.

"There's no Tricia," I said, as though I'd expected him to know that all along. "That's just an icebreaker I use with the young hotties. Makes me sound in-demand, and gets 'em thinking about me as an option."

"That works?"

"I have four girls ready to come home with me. What do you think?"

"You swear they won't be disappointed when they find out I'm the friend you're bringing?"

"I swear. They'll be thrilled. They'll be all over you." I frowned. "One thing, though. The blue haired girl? Taylor? She's mine. I love those big doe eyes of hers."

"But *I* want Taylor though," he said, talking about her like she was a toy in a store window. No, this guy was not a winner in any sense of the word.

"Too bad," I said. "She's mine."

"She's mine, or I'm not coming." He folded his arms in finality.

I sighed.

"Fine. You're being a jerk, but fine. Let's go."

His face lit up so bright I probably saw what he looked like when he was a kid on Christmas morning.

*"I'll thank you not to mention the c-word, if you please," Eamon said.*

Sorry. Point is, we made our way out of that mall. And that guy probably never moved that fast before in his life.

---

*"*L*et's get another round,*" S*ebastian said.*

*"Fine," Eamon allowed, "but stay focused. We're getting somewhere."*

*Clark came by. Brought more drinks. Took away more glasses. Parked himself back behind the bar, where he'd been doing something with his computer all afternoon.*

Only a few people in the parking lot, when the fortysomething guy and I got out there. The afternoon sun was getting hotter, and the smell of warm asphalt was comforting after the fried smell of the food court.

Traffic noises in the background were louder. More people not very far away, racing down I5 to their homes in Wilsonville or Salem from their Portland jobs.

The few people in the parking lot paid no attention to us. They were either busy loading their cars, or hustling into the mall for something or other.

What there was *not*, however, was a group of four girls waiting by my truck. When he noticed this, the fortysomething guy frowned at me.

"Hey," he said. "What gives? Where are they?"

"Look…" I frowned. "What's your name, anyway? Won't look good if I don't know it."

"Fisher," he said, eying me suspiciously again.

"Well, Fisher, I'm Hank Habersham," I said. "Pleased to make your acquaintance. And I thought you were a man of the world."

*"Ha," Sebastian said, making the other two smile.*

"I am," Fisher said defensively.

"Then you know girls are never on time," I said with a smile and a clap on his shoulder.

His shoulder was wetter than I'd like. He had flop sweat going over the possibility of actual sex with another human being — just the kind of cute girls he'd always wanted but probably never even approached — and the combination of excitement and nerves wasn't doing anything good for his stench.

"Look," I said with a smile. "They're probably in the bathroom right now, making themselves pretty for us. Let's wait for them in the truck."

"In the truck?" He sounded more unsure than suspicious, but I was getting awful tired of his questions. I had an agenda to keep.

"Fisher," I said, clapping him on the shoulder again and looking him in the eye. "You'll look cooler if you're already sitting when they approach. More in-control."

"Yeah?" he smiled, like he liked that image of himself.

Oh. Smiling was a bad move for this guy. His teeth were gray. Old Fisher probably hadn't been to a dentist in far, far too long.

I swear. Even if I didn't sacrifice this guy, I'd be doing him a favor by killing him.

"Yeah," I said, keeping that smile firmly in place. "Besides. I can turn on the AC. Don't want to be sweating when the girls get here."

"Hey, good thought, Hank."

And with that he finally — *finally* — got in the fucking truck.

I was muttering under my breath about idiots in general and Fisher in particular, but training was training. I glanced about. Pretending to be looking for the girls, but making sure no one was paying any special attention to us.

Good thing I did.

About six rows away. Gray Toyota Avalon. Trunk had been open when Fisher and I came out of the mall. At the time, a young couple had been loading bags into that trunk.

They were out of bags, but the trunk was still open.

Got that warning flutter at the back of my neck.

Paid them a little more notice as my eyes tracked past them.

Mid-twenties. Fit. And I don't just mean fit as in they weren't fat like so many people these days. I mean fit like they were regulars at their local gym, and in between workouts ran half-marathons.

They had a Germanic look to them.

*"Did they," Eamon said, but not like it was a question.*

The blonde and blue-eyed thing. But at the time, I was more concerned about what the woman did when I had that glance.

Now, when I spotted them, they were both looking into their trunk. Meaning I saw them in profile. But the woman, she looked away as my eyes passed over them.

And she was talking into a phone.

Coincidence? Maybe. But I couldn't afford to take the risk.

I slipped the syringe out of my pocket as I opened my driver's side door. Concealed it in my hand.

The cab of my truck felt too close as I sat down. And not just because of Fisher's stench. I just wasn't used to having a second big man in there with me. Drove alone too much.

Fisher, though, he was smiling. Giddy. Starting to believe this was really going to happen.

I gave him a smile, to get him looking my way. Idiot shot me a thumbs-up.

Instead of returning it, I nodded back toward the mall, smiled wider, and said, "Here they come now."

He whipped his head around.

I stuck him in the jugular with the syringe and gave him the full load.

He made a series of pained, whimpering sounds. But all that excitement worked against him. Rocketed the tranq through his system.

He'd barely gotten out the words, "What are you..." before his eyes started fluttering. Couldn't keep them open.

I already had the engine cranked. I pulled out of my parking space nice and smooth, but trying to watch everywhere at once.

I needed to keep an eye on that Avalon. The couple wasn't standing at their trunk anymore. They were getting in their car.

I tried to use sight lines against them, but the parking lot was just too empty.

I had a bit of a lead on them, if they were following me. Enough that I had a slim chance to lose them. Problem was, if I did, I'd soon have a drooling, unconscious Fisher leaning against his side window.

Sure, right now he was still limply flopping about and bubbling little sounds that were probably intended as wild protests. But that wouldn't last.

He'd either end up drooling on my lap or the side window. And people might notice something that disgusting. Which was why I had the tarp ready for him in the first place.

But if I took the time to cover him with the tarp, the Avalon would have time to catch me.

If it was following me.

Had to compromise.

I pulled around the other side of the mall, into the older parking structure — the one with four levels of aging concrete, two of which were underground — and sped my way past empty spaces down to the bottom.

I parked across three spaces, with my truck concealed behind a huge concrete pylon.

Fisher was actually still fighting for consciousness. I slugged him a couple of times to help him fall asleep. Then I tucked him down and covered him with the tarp. Might have some trouble getting fresh air, but that would help keep him out.

While I was down there and presumably unobserved — at least, I didn't see any cameras, and I checked — I wiped my prints off the syringe and threw it to shatter off in a corner.

I was back behind the wheel and just about to pull out when I heard tires on concrete. I turned and saw headlights coming down the ramp.

Excitement sizzled through my veins. If that was the Avalon, I might lose them yet.

The question was — speed or silence?

No. If I were them, I'd have my windows down, trying to hear everything I could. And with the eight cylinders under my hood, they'd probably hear me even if I idled.

And idling would've been too slow anyway.

I punched it.

My engine roared, and my truck leapt forward. Tires squealed around a tight corner and I took that ramp like I expected to jump at the end.

The Avalon's engine was quieter than mine. But I heard it all the same.

The chase was on.

The chase lasted exactly three blocks. Then I was stuck, first in line waiting eight eternal minutes while a freight train rolled through downtown Tualatin. I was surrounded by the early commute traffic, too. No chance I could open up the engine and really lose that Avalon.

I had my window down, so the smell of warm asphalt and gasoline could diminish Fisher's stench. Made the sounds of traffic and the train louder, as well as the dinging railroad crossing signal.

The Avalon was back behind me a ways. Maybe twelve cars back. The man behind the wheel, but it looked as though he was playing with his dashboard. His GPS maybe. And the woman was in the passenger seat, still on the phone.

Still on the phone?

Fuck.

All right. A calming breath didn't calm me much, but I always do better under pressure anyway.

The woman was on the phone. So odds were pretty good she was coordinating with somebody.

*"How'd they find you?" Zed asked.*

Believe me, I was wondering that too. I'll get to the answer later.

Right then, I knew that if the woman was coordinating with others, then the guy had to be using his GPS to try to find a place to trap me. Or at least predict where I was going.

Figured that gave me an edge.

Another part of being a hunter is knowing your terrain. And I knew Tualatin better than most of its residents.

Soon as the train was gone and the bar was up, I shot across the street and crossed a lane to pull into a strip mall parking lot. Yeah, the guy I cut off laid into his horn, but he didn't matter.

Around the back of the strip mall was a narrow driveway that led down a long alley between two rows of apartment buildings. It's an alley that doesn't appear on the local maps, mostly because the only people who use it are the apartment dwellers who need access to their parking spaces. And, of course, garbagemen.

Couldn't go too fast down that alley. And not just because it was full of potholes. Too much chance of some kid with a ball zipping around a parked car. And the last thing I needed was to kill somebody on my way to a human sacrifice.

No sign of the Avalon in my rearview mirror. They might not've been able to cut over in time to get into that strip mall parking lot. And even if they did, they might miss that little driveway, figuring I'd take the wider, smoother street for my getaway.

I was just reaching the last apartment building when I heard a gunshot and my tire blew out.

Truck jerked to my right. Straight toward the concrete wall protecting a Dumpster.

I yanked the steering wheel to spare my bumper and airbags.

Felt a bee sting on my neck.

I swiped at it. Knocked something away.

I braked at the end of the driveway. Heart pounding. My mouth tasted like aluminum.

T-intersection, on a block full of houses and small apartment buildings. I checked both ways. Street was pretty quiet. Just some hired hand mowing a lawn a few houses down.

Tingling started in my fingers and toes.

I needed to change my tire. That was all. I knew that. Had a spare in the back of the truck. Always did. I'd have to move some hickory logs ... for it...

I shook my head.

Hickory logs. Did I have enough hickory logs for tonight?

That was a stupid question. Of course ... of course I did...

Didn't I?

Something was off.

No. *Everything* was off. Like I was separated from the world by a layer of bubble wrap.

I reached for my door handle and almost pulled into the street. Jerked the truck to a stop. Slammed on the emergency brake.

Reached for the door handle. Missed.

Wait. Now there were two door handles. And they were spinning.

No. Not just the door handles. Everything was spinning.

A warning klaxon finally went off in my head, but it was too late. My system couldn't even kick up any adrenaline to help me fight the effects of what had obviously not been a bee sting.

Now, I don't know about you guys, but I've been drugged before. And this wasn't usually how it worked.

Usually, I recognize it earlier. My body kicks in the adrenals, and I fight like hell.

But sitting there behind the wheel of my truck, no adrenaline came to my aid.

No need to fight ripped through me.

I started worrying again that I hadn't cut enough hickory, as the world began to tunnel down on me into blackness.

Then, well, there were two unconscious people in the cab of my truck.

***

My mind came to before my body did.

I was breathing. I knew that because I could hear the slow rise and fall of my chest. Couldn't feel it, though, any more than I could tell if I was sitting up or lying down.

Disconcerting sensation, let me tell you.

My breathing didn't sound especially wet or dry, so I figured that was a good thing.

I could hear wood creaking. My first though was a kitchen chair. I wasn't sitting in it, though. Sound was too far away. My best guess was maybe three steps away, someone was sitting. Watching me. And adjusting their position, while waiting for me to wake.

I was breathing through my nose. Figured that was a good thing too. I smelled sawdust. And some grease. Something else, too. Fried cheese, maybe?

Couldn't make myself breathe through my mouth, so I couldn't taste the air. Probably wouldn't have helped. I could still taste that aluminum taste from earlier. Probably from the drugs.

Taste, though. Taste was good. Meant more of my nerves were waking up.

Still. Right now I was awake, even if I didn't look it. And though I didn't have the resources of my body, I did have my mind.

I started to slip out of my body. What Eamon would call "astral projection," but my folks always just called it "sending."

It didn't work.

*"What do you mean, 'it didn't work?'" Eamon said.*

I mean I attempted to send my consciousness outward but I couldn't do it. I was penned inside my body.

Which told me I was bound, and that there were spells of some kind on the bindings.

All right. Didn't mean I was helpless.

There's a spell we know that should break magical bindings. Calls on both Yog Sothoth and Nyarlathotep, both of whom are perfect for that sort of thing.

Yes, sir, I've used that spell at least a dozen separate times and never had it fail once.

Not until yesterday, as I sat or lay there with only my mind to work with.

I'd like to say the problem was that I couldn't even mumble the incantation, but that wasn't it.

No. Whatever they'd done to bind me, I was cut off from outside resources. Yog Sothoth and Nyarlathotep couldn't help me, because I couldn't reach out to them. Not past whatever bound me.

No help there.

So I did the only thing I could do. I sent my consciousness all through my body. Working to bring my body back as fast and as thoroughly as possible.

No doubt they'd expect me to come around slowly. Need time to pull myself together. But with my mind whisking through my muscles and sinew, prompting my organs and pushing the distribution of my circulatory system, I'd come to fully myself and ready to fight.

Couldn't tell you how long it took exactly. Didn't have the kind of input I'd need for that.

I do know that by the time I raised my head, I had my heart beating good and strong, and my adrenals flowing like beer at one of Sebastian's parties.

I was tied to a solid steel chair, that had been bolted to the concrete beneath me. My arms were tied behind me at the elbow. My hands were crossed and tied at the wrist. That wrist binding was also hooked to the chair somehow.

My legs were spread across the cold, steel seat. My knees and ankles were separately bound to the chair legs.

The bindings were tight enough to keep me from working myself loose, but *just* loose enough not to cut off my circulation.

Whoever had bound me knew what they were doing.

I snapped my eyes open.

Dim lighting from a pair of bare, incandescent bulbs that dangled from the ceiling on wires.

I could see the ropes now, and the spells written into them, trapping me even tighter than mere physical restraints.

These guys knew what they were doing all right.

They had me in someone's concrete basement. Cold. Storage boxes had all been moved off into one corner. Maybe a dozen of them.

At the other end of the basement — which was pretty big, maybe half a basketball court — some wood and metalworking tools, and the power tools to go with them. There were more and better lights above that part of the basement, but those lights were off.

Spare steel lay on a workbench. Enough to make a second chair...

Between me and all those tools, a black guy was sitting and watching me. Very dark skin. Tight-cropped hair. He wore a purple shirt with a collar, looked like silk maybe, and black slacks and shoes.

He *was* sitting on a kitchen chair, by the way. Not that it made me feel better, knowing I'd been right.

"This some kind of reverse KKK thing?" I asked, knowing it wasn't. "You kidnap rednecks and lynch 'em?"

"I happen to know that four members of your cult are African American," he said in a high, smooth voice. "So don't try playing the good-old-boy-racist card thinking to anger me into making a mistake. I won't."

All right. That was bad. That he knew that about our membership was almost as bad as that he had me here at all. Private bunch like us, we only gather for ... well, we don't just get together to go bowling.

If this guy knew that much about my cult, he probably knew a whole hell of a lot.

"So what's the deal then?" I asked, trying to make it sound like a joke. "Torture me hoping for information, then slit my throat and throw my body to the coyotes when I don't cooperate?"

He smiled. Shook his head.

"I'm not going to harm you, Mister..." He frowned. "Now, do you prefer..." and the son of a bitch listed four of my favorite aliases.

I didn't answer.

"Fine then," he said with a mild shrug. "I'll just call you Harley."

That was enough to break out a bead of sweat on my forehead. None of my aliases used that name.

"And what should I call you?"

He smiled again. "Do you need me to say it?"

"Carter."

"Very good. Now that the introductions are over, I didn't bring you here to hurt you, and I didn't bring you here for information. You see, if I ask you a question, then I'm telling you what I don't know yet. And there's very little about your little group that I don't know."

Oh, this guy was good. But he wasn't *that* good.

"Oh, maybe you've found a directory," I said with a smile. "And maybe you've done some digging around about me, personally. But if you really knew that much, I wouldn't be *here* right now. Would I?"

The Carters didn't know where our ritual site was. They'd managed a lot, but they hadn't broken through our hiding spells. If they had, if they knew, they'd have hit us there. Stopped the ritual and ruined the site in one swift move.

And this guy and me, we both knew it.

He chuckled appreciatively.

"We found your sacrifice, though, didn't we?" He smiled. "And gee, we stopped you from bringing in a backup, didn't we? Have to admit, though, I didn't think that big guy would be your type. Not from what I've seen on your various social media accounts."

"So what's the plan?" I asked, trying to sound bored while inside I was churning like a bear caught in a trap. "You don't want information, what do you want?"

"We have what we want," he said, then gave me a smug smile. "Sometimes, all that is necessary for good to triumph is for evil men to do ... nothing. And I'd say we've made sure of that. For tonight, at least."

The son of a bitch actually gave me a moment to respond. But all I could think about was how red his eyes would get if I could only strangle him.

That didn't stop him from talking some more.

"Your sacrifice, Fisher, is recovering nicely and will get home safe and sound tonight. And with you here, and no sacrifice, no ritual to raise R'lyeh."

He was fishing. Hoping for confirmation. Had to be. No way he knew what we were planning. So I tried playing it dumb.

"To raise what now? We were going to—"

"Nice try," he said, and shook his head. "You aren't the only ones watching the conjunctions across more than one world."

He leaned a little closer. "Want me to tell you exactly what time you were hoping to spill Fisher's blood? Because I know."

I started struggling then, but it was no good. He had me. And he knew it.

There was nothing I could do.

15

——————

## CLARK

HARLEY DOWNED DAMN NEAR A FULL GLASS GUINNESS WITHOUT stopping. Slammed the glass down on the table and called out to me, "Another!"

"Maybe you should..." Eamon started to caution, but Harley shook him off and waved his glass at me.

I pulled him a fresh one, and when Sebastian nodded at me, holding up his own empty, I pulled one for him too.

Me, the entire time I was getting those last beers and bringing them out, I was fizzing inside like antacid tablets.

Carters. So. That African American guy, the one in the purple shirt. He'd been a Carter. I still wasn't sure if it was a name or a title, but now, I mean...

The guy sounded so cool. So together. So organized. He had Harley's number. Stopped the world from ending last night.

Sounded like the kind of guy who could, say, protect a local bar owner who came to him with information...

But even thinking things like that felt dangerous. As though one or more of the gruesome foursome could read my mind. Would know what I was planning, and would stop me in the worst way possible.

So I tried to hold myself as steady as possible while I delivered those drinks. Tried to ignore the way my heart was racing, and pretend that I wasn't sweating despite the AC.

Eamon and Zed were focused on Harley, and Harley was focused on his beer. Sebastian, though, may have noticed.

Maybe not, though. He always eyed me when I brought them drinks or food. So maybe I was just being paranoid.

Either way, I got back behind the bar as fast as I could, without rushing. And those last five feet seemed to take me five hours.

Then I was back, as safe as I ever was, behind my bar and my laptop. And once I was, they started talking again.

"Not sure how long he kept me there," Harley said at last. "I know that he sat there watching me for what had to have been hours. His attention never flagged. Not once."

"Did he have any more to say?" Zed asked.

"He'd talk to me if I wanted to talk," Harley said with a sigh, "but I couldn't figure out much of anything from him."

"Did he crack your phone?"

"Didn't even try," Harley said. "Safeguards on it were all still in place, and the phone was in my pocket where it was supposed to be."

"How did he let you go?"

"An alarm went off on his phone. He nodded. Went over to the workbenches. There he picked up a blowgun and shot me in the neck with another tranq."

Harley downed a third of his beer. "I woke up around three in the morning. Alone in my truck, which was parked back on the side street next to the driveway where they'd caught me. Tarp folded on the seat next to me. My own spare tire on my right front."

"No sign of a pyramid?" Sebastian asked. "Or anything that might tie this to a splinter of the old Illuminati?"

"I wouldn't have thought so," Harley said, "except—"

"The Germanic couple," Eamon said

Harley nodded. "That guy you mentioned. Klaus. From the description you gave him, he might be brothers with the guy who was driving the Avalon."

"Lots of people look Germanic," Zed said, "doesn't mean they're brothers."

"Doesn't mean they're not," Harley said. "And considering that the same group appears to have come after you three, it stands to reason that they were also helping the Carters with my cult."

"What kind of coven worth its blood would work with the Carters?" Eamon asked, sounding as though the words tasted sour.

"The kind who think they can clear out the competition," Zed said, "then lay low for a while before moving with expected impunity."

"So they've never dealt with Carters before," Eamon said.

"It does seem tenuous," Zed admitted.

"Enough of a connection for an alliance?" Sebastian asked.

Harley raised his glass. "Enough that I damned well want to make sure one way or the other. So yes."

All four of them said, "Allied," and clinked and drank.

"Have anything to go on?" Eamon asked.

"License number and VIN of that Avalon," Harley said.

"You got the VIN?" Sebastian asked in disbelief. Which made me happy, 'cause I couldn't have asked.

"I haven't been to bed yet," Harley said, "and I'm not without some resources of my own."

"Then the next step—" Eamon started, but Zed cut him off with raised hands.

"The next step," he said, "is to settle up here and get moving. We have a lot to do."

"Right," Harley said. And they all clinked again and drained their glasses before throwing down more than enough cash to cover all their drinks and food, and still leave me a pretty darned good tip.

They started filing out.

"Good as always, Clark," Eamon said.

Harley and Zed just nodded at me.

"Always a pleasure," Sebastian said, trailing a little behind them.

I watched them cross the floor. Open the door. They were almost gone. I was almost ready to take a relaxing breath and figure out my own next move.

But then Sebastian said, "Be with you in a sec, guys. Forgot something."

"Hurry," Harley called after him, but the other three went out while Sebastian hustled back into the bar.

He didn't go back to his table, though. He came up to me. Smiled at me from across the bar.

"You, er, forgot something?" I asked, trying to think, which wasn't easy while looking Sebastian in the eye.

"The other three," he said softly, "they don't think much of my sect and our magic. But I read people better than the rest of those three combined."

"Oh?" I asked, openly sweating now and hoping he couldn't hear my heart pounding the way I could. Then again, it was pounding so hard he could probably feel the beat through the bar.

"Right now," he said softly, "you're asking yourself, 'Should I go find the Carters?' Because I think that today you realized, for the first time, that we're not like one of your roleplaying groups."

I swallowed. "You're not?"

He shook his head, holding my eyes the entire time.

"We like meeting here," he said. "I like your daiquiris, and we all like your food. We like the ambiance. And we do well by you, don't we? Good tips? Maybe a free keg of Guinness?"

"That was..." I cleared my throat. "You mean..."

"You know full well I got you that keg," he said. "Absolutely free. Just like the advice I'm about to give you. Forget what you heard us talk about today. Forget the Carters. You just keep cooking food and making drinks."

I started to say something. He silenced me with fingers against my lips.

"You can eavesdrop all you want. I don't mind." He smiled, and damn if my heart didn't skip a beat even though I was all but petrified with fear. "I kind of like it. But if you ever move against us, we will end you in ways you can't even imagine."

He let those words hang in the air for just a moment.

"And in case you're thinking, 'Well, if the Carters take care of you, I don't have to worry.' Yes. You do. Because even if we can't avenge ourselves, we *will* be avenged."

He fluttered his lashes at me.

"And you know I'm not lying, don't you?"

I had to clear my throat, which had suddenly gone dry. "Yes."

"You know how much our kind of people enjoy vengeance, don't you?"

"Yes."

"So when I leave here, what are you going to do?"

Now that was the real trick question. Because the thing was, everything he was saying just convinced me more and more that I needed to find these Carters.

The gruesome foursome were just too powerful to be ignored. If these Carters could stop them, then I needed to find them.

Yeah, it was risky. But some risks were worth taking.

Still. To get through the next five minutes, I had to say something that would suit the overwhelming fear coursing through my system.

"Work my shift," I said, "best I can, anyway. Then go home and huddle in a tiny ball until I can think straight."

"Oh," Sebastian said, sounding sad, but his eyes were still smiling. "We can't have that. Not from our favorite bartender."

He reached across the bar and pulled me into a kiss.

I'd like to think it was just the shock that made me let him.

But that kiss, it wasn't erotic. He wasn't turning me on. No. In some ways, it was worse.

That kiss was calming. Warm, soothing relaxation spread from my lips all through me until I felt as though I'd just woken up on a warm spring morning, surrounded by comfy blankets and pillows, with the certainty that the universe loved me and nothing bad could ever happen.

When the kiss broke and I pulled back, confused, Sebastian was smiling and muttering something I couldn't understand.

Finally, he spoke louder.

"Now. Feel all better about everything you've heard today?"

And damn it, I did. I felt good. Happy. And I wasn't worried in the least about what I'd heard, or what might happen to the Carters, whoever they were.

Those things, they weren't my problems. My problems were mundane, real things. Earning enough to keep the bar going while still making my mortgage payments. Whether or not Cindy and I should try being more than casual.

The rest of what I'd heard today, well, I didn't know if it was real or not anyway, did I? I mean, stuff like that just didn't happen.

Magic wasn't real. Everyone knew that.

Sebastian nodded, smiling wider now.

"Have a good week, Clark," he said. "See you next Wednesday!"

"Bye, Sebastian." Normally I'd've wished him a good week, but even feeling good as I was, that would have been going too far.

I did watch him walk away, though. And even that didn't bother me. So what if I found him attractive? Who wouldn't?

Then the door closed behind him and he was gone.

***

SEBASTIAN WASN'T GONE SIXTY SECONDS BEFORE THERE WAS A KNOCK AT the back door of Zoth.

I'd like to think that, somewhere deep inside me, I knew that was weird, and maybe a little worried.

Most of me was still feeling good from that kiss, though, so I didn't even hesitate to go around the bar and head back.

I was smiling when I pulled open the bar door.

Before I could even see who was there, I heard a harsh puff of breath, and a cloud of white dust hit me full in the face.

I staggered backwards. Managed to keep my feet until I reached a table I could grab and keep from falling.

I faced that table, breathing hard. Shaking my head.

Whatever Sebastian had done to me, it was gone.

I felt the full terror, again, of realizing that four evil wizards had been meeting in my bar, making their evil plans.

I turned around.

There stood Petey. Still in his Guinness uniform.

"Take a seat there, Clark," Petey said, and eased me into a chair with a strong grip. "Breathe. Don't forget to breathe. Want me to get you some water? A beer maybe?"

I shook my head, frowning at him.

"What did they tell you?" he said, taking the seat next to me and shaking my shoulder in his urgency. "Tell me everything."

"You," I said, frowning deeper as pieces came together in my head. "You mean, you're a—"

"Don't say it," he said quickly, covering my mouth with a hand that smelled like sausage. "Your speculations don't matter to them. They know you're not a player. But knowledge, that's different. If they feel knowledge and certainty from you, they'll pry out the rest. And they'll do it when we can't get to you in time. Which means you're *fucked*. Got me?"

I nodded. He took his hand away.

"I could use some water now."

Petey hustled to get it. Waited impatiently, drumming his fingers, until I was ready to talk.

I told him everything I could think of. Everything I heard. Nothing I guessed. He didn't want that.

At least, I don't *think* I told him my guesses. Hard to be sure, at that point. And I'm pretty sure I forgot a few things.

But the time I finished, he was smiling.

"Good. Very good," he said, and clapped me on the shoulder. "You've been a big help."

"Good," I said with a frown. I was pretty sure I was doing the right thing, but I didn't know for sure that Petey was a Carter, and I couldn't know or I wouldn't be able to help.

Which was what he might tell me if he was just a rival cultist. And I had no way to find out.

But then, Petey'd been my Guinness guy for two years, and he'd never done wrong by me, and he'd never given me any reason to think he was evil.

So weird, that my life had come to that.

"All right," he said. Then looked me over, nodded, and said it again. "All right, Clark. I'm going to ask you something, and I just want an honest answer. All right?"

I nodded.

"Would you be willing to report like this every week?"

"They'd kill me. And I'm not sure they'd stop there."

"They'll never know." He pulled out a little unlabeled medicine bottle, the kind with a dropped for the top. "Put three drops of this in a glass of water before they're due to arrive. *Drink the whole glass of water.* Do that, and you'll be good and relaxed through the whole time they're here, no matter what they talk about."

"But Sebastian—"

"Even Sebastian will never suspect a thing."

"You promise?"

"I swear."

I nodded. He handed me the bottle. "Obviously, don't let them see the bottle."

"Right," I said.

"Okay," he said, then clapped his hands once. "All right. I need to go to work. See you next week, Clark."

I nodded a goodbye, and Petey moved to the door.

"Wait," I said. "About that keg—"

"Don't ask questions you don't want to know the answers to," Petey said. Then smiled and left.

I sat there for a moment. Wondering if I'd just gotten caught up in some kind of cosmic battle. Wondering almost as much if I'd just been the target of an elaborate practical joke.

Either way, I was thoroughly outclassed.

Whatever was going on out there, it was way, *way* too big for me.

So I went into the bathroom and pulled myself together.

I had a bar to run.

# SIGN UP FOR STEFON'S NEWSLETTER

Stefon loves to keep in touch with his readers, and loves to keep you reading. The best way for him to do both is for you to sign up for his newsletter.

Sign up at http://www.stefonmears.com/join

If you sign up for Stefon's newsletter, you get...

- Monthly updates about his publishing and travel schedules
- His latest news, in brief, and answers to reader questions
- A free short story for signing up
- List-only offers and occasional specials
- Plus a free short story every month!

# ABOUT THE AUTHOR

Stefon Mears has had offers to join some pretty dicey cults, but avoided them so far. Stefon has more than thirty books to his credit, and he never stops writing. He earned his M.F.A. in Creative Writing from N.I.L.A., and his B.A. in Religious Studies (double emphasis in Ritual and Mythology) from U.C. Berkeley. He's a lifelong gamer and fantasy fan. Stefon lives in Portland, Oregon, with his wife and three cats.

*Look for Stefon online:*
www.stefonmears.com
himself@stefonmears.com